Foul Play

Foul Play

Janet Evanovich

(Originally published under the name Steffie Hall)

An Imprint of HarperCollinsPublishers

FIRST HARPERLUXE EDITION

HarperLuxe™ is a trademark of HarperCollins Publishers

ISBN: 978-0-06-171328-6

08 09 10 11 12 ID/RRD 10 9 8 7 6 5 4 3 2 1

To Kenneth Wright . . .
veterinarian extraordinaire
and the best friend a beagle ever had.

Chapter 1

Jacob Elliott flipped his left-turn signal on and patiently waited for Mrs. Moyer to pull out of her parking space. He knew it was Mrs. Moyer because her dog, Harold, was frantically clawing at the back window of her station wagon. Jacob Elliott was not especially good at remembering people, but he never forgot a dog. He was debating the merits of this peculiarity when a gleaming, cherry-red sports car zipped around the corner and beat him out of Mrs. Moyer's spot.

The red car door instantly flew open. Two shapely legs extended themselves from the driver's side, and a delicate blonde emerged. She threw her hands into the air in a gesture of furious exasperation and gave the door a thunderous slam, catching the hem of her swirly pink skirt in the jaws of the powerful machine. She glared at the skirt contemptuously, gave a yank, and tore herself loose—leaving half a yard of pink material held hostage by the car. Without even so much as a backward glance she flounced off to the supermarket, fists clenched, eyes narrowed, nose defiantly tipped upward.

Jacob Elliott sat wide-eyed and slack jawed in disbelief as the glossy blond curls disappeared behind the automatic glass doors. He felt a smile creep into the corners of his mouth and a disturbing rush of heat burn across his belly. He was in love.

Life, Amy Klasse fumed, was not fair. You do all the right things, and *bam*! You get kicked in the teeth. It made her furious, especially since innocent children were going to be among the hapless victims.

Wrenching a wire cart out of the cart stack, she viciously pushed it toward the vegetables. She glared at her shredded skirt. Of all the lousy luck; now, on top of everything else, she'd ruined her favorite outfit. Darn that car. And it wasn't as if she could afford to buy another pink skirt: She was unemployed. She'd been unemployed for twenty minutes. She looked at her watch. No, make that thirty-five minutes. All because of a chicken. A *chicken*, for crying out loud! She muttered a well-chosen expletive and indiscriminately grabbed a grapefruit from a huge display. "A chicken!" she exclaimed, thunking her fist against her forehead.

Jake watched in absolute astonishment as his new-found love flung a grapefruit into her cart and took off in a blind rage. The remaining grapefruits hesitated for a moment in precarious limbo, and then hurled them-selves onto the floor like so many lemmings making the final, fatal, migration. Jake stopped a grapefruit with the side of his foot and flipped it into the air, like a soccer ball. He scooped up several more and carefully lined them up in their bin.

From the corner of his eye he caught the infuriated blonde heading for the fresh eggs. "Oh, no," he said, groaning, "not the eggs."

In silent horror, he watched as she chose a carton and in some magical way managed to grasp only the top lid, spilling the entire dozen eggs into the immaculate glass case. The eggs instantly exploded on their companions, oozing across gleaming shelves, sliming into pristine crevices.

The blonde stared at the eggs as if they were aliens. She shook her head and muttered something indiscern-ible while Jake doubled over his own cart in an attempt to abort the laughter that was rising in his throat.

In his entire life he'd never come across a female who was that outraged, that clumsy, and that sexy.

She wasn't sexy by centerfold standards, but there was definitely something about her that increased his heart rate. He liked the way her short blond curls bounced when she walked. He liked her peaches-and-cream coloring and her wide cornflower blue eyes, and the way she carried her slight frame. And most of all, Jake was intrigued by the intensity of her fury, the way she could muster her pride and walk away from disaster. She was not a woman whose life would be ruined by a broken fingernail.

A stockboy appeared with a mop and sponge. "Don't worry about it," he told Amy. "Happens all the time."

Amy nodded numbly. Lord, what a mess. Those eggs were like her life—scrambled. She decided she didn't want eggs anyway. Eggs reminded her of chickens; and you know what chickens do—they steal people's jobs!

She proceeded down the aisles at a much more cautious pace, selecting fixings for a spaghetti dinner. She intended to go home, brew up some of her fantastic spaghetti sauce, and eat until she burst. Then she would sit in front of the TV and make the most of feeling sorry for herself. She hefted a bag of cat litter into her cart and continued on.

Jake saw the tear in the bottom of the litter bag. He could have told her. He could have introduced himself and explained that she was leaving a trail of cat litter that wound its way through the bulk-food section and staunchly marched through sanitary products, but he didn't. It was much more fun to observe her at a distance and follow the granules.

Besides, he knew when he would make his move. Calamity Jane didn't have a purse, and there were no pockets that he could see in her bedraggled skirt. His guess was that she'd gone off in such a huff that she'd left her money behind. He pursued her at a leisurely pace, selecting a bottle of burgundy to accompany her spaghetti dinner and adding a frozen pie for dessert.

He lined up behind his quarry at the checkout, feeling an unsettling surge of affection for her while his anxiety ran amok. What if his plan didn't work? What if she was married? She didn't have a ring on her finger, but that was no guarantee. Maybe she lost her ring this morning when she was bathing the baby.

He peered over her shoulder and warily watched the fresh mushrooms and sweet peppers glide along the belt. She'd probably burned down three kitchens and poisoned countless men. Could that be why she wasn't wearing a ring? Most likely she'd killed her husband—accidentally run him over with her flashy red car. Maybe he should reconsider . . . Nah.

The checker smiled at Amy. "Forty-three dollars and seventy-six cents."

Amy froze. No purse. There was a sweep of momentary panic until she mentally retraced her steps and assured herself the purse was safely stowed in her locker at the station. This is what happens when you lose control of your emotions, she thought. You make an idiot of yourself in the supermarket.

Jake waited. Timing was everything. You couldn't look too eager when you were picking women up at the supermarket like this. Not that he'd ever done it before, but he just knew you had to be cool about these things.

Amy pressed her lips together in dismay. "I'm sorry. I don't have my purse with me."

Now. Jake leaned forward. "Is there a problem?" Lord, she smelled wonderful when you got this close to her. Sweet, like honeysuckle, he thought. And her voice was clear and musical. Her laughter would be like that, too, he decided.

The checker looked unconcerned. "She forgot her purse."

"Oh." Steady, Elliott, he cautioned. Subtlety, that's the key word. You have to be subtle. He turned his big soft brown eyes to Amy. "Do you live far away? Maybe you can call someone to bring the money. A neighbor?" Slight pause. "Your husband?" Clever, he thought, very clever. Hold your breath . . .

She looked despondent. "I just moved into the neighborhood. I don't know anyone, and I don't have a husband."

Whew! She didn't have a husband. Jake tried to control the smile that was twitching across his mouth. "Maybe I can help. I'd be happy to loan you the money."

"That's very nice of you, but I couldn't let you do that. You don't even know me."

Jake studied her flushed face, allowing his gaze to roam from her cap of shiny curls to her slightly up-turned nose and kissable bow-shaped mouth. Her neck was smooth and elegant, her breasts small and round. His gaze lingered at the torn skirt, wondering at the slender legs hidden within. "That's true. I don't know you, and you do look a little . . . um, unkempt."

Amy looked down at her skirt. "It was my car. It ate my skirt."

Jake nodded sympathetically. He glanced at the bags of groceries sitting in her cart. "I'll tell you what, I'll make a deal with you. It looks to me like you've got the makings of a spaghetti dinner there. As you can see"—he pointed to his cartful of TV dinners—"my culinary skills stop at defrosting. I'll pay for your food, if you'll make me a home-cooked meal. Fair?"

Now it was Amy's turn to take a long hard look at Jacob Elliott, six feet tall with broad shoulders, slim hips, and running shoes held together with surgical tape. A few crisp black hairs curled from the open neck of his shirt. His sleeves had been rolled to the elbow, displaying strong corded forearms, and Amy guessed that the shirt hid muscles in all the right places. He was perfectly yummy. Coffee-colored hair waved over his eyes and along his neck, giving him a slightly rugged look, which was substantiated by a five o'clock shadow. Perfect teeth flashed white against a dashing smile any pirate would have been proud to own.

Amy felt a shiver run along her spine and instinctively checked to make sure her blouse was buttoned. "I don't think so," she answered, trying to ignore the fact that her mouth had gone dry as sand.

The checkout clerk shook her head in disbelief. "What a ninny."

Amy felt her jaw drop. "I beg your pardon?"

The older woman stood with her hand on her hip and grinned. "Wouldn't catch me turning down a chance to cook *his* dinner."

"I don't know this man. He could be an axe murderer."

"Honey, this is Dr. Elliott. Everyone knows Dr. Elliott. He owns the veterinary clinic just around the corner."

The checker one aisle over leaned across her cash register. "Dr. Elliott saved Sarah Maxwell's cat when it was run over by a truck. Cat was a terrible mess, but

Dr. Elliott worked on that poor little thing and stitched it together like new."

"And Frannie Newfarmer's beagle," a woman two carts behind Amy added. "He nursed her beagle back to health when it was poisoned by the gardening service. Dr. Elliott slept in the office every night for almost a week, watching over that dog, till he was sure the little fella would live."

Jacob Elliott smiled down at Amy. "See, you can trust me."

Not by the hairs on your chinny chin chin, she thought. There was unmistakable mischief in his liquid brown eyes—bedroom eyes. And his wide mouth had a sensual curve to it that went straight to the pit of her stomach. He might be great at saving beagles, but she'd bet he was hell on single women. "I don't live far from here," Amy explained. "I'll drive home and get some money."

Jake slouched against his cart, counting the seconds until she realized her keys were locked in her car. When the startled expression appeared in her eyes he calmly paid for both their groceries and escorted her to the parking lot. "The large jeep-type vehicle," he told her. "The purple job with the big black dog."

Amy stumbled slightly at the sight of the "purple job." It was big and square, more maroon than purple, splattered with mud and riddled with rust. A coat hanger antenna zigzagged crazily from the hood, and a bashed-in rear bumper sported a faded sticker that read HAVE YOU HUGGED YOUR VETERINARIAN TODAY? She'd never been one to look a gift horse in the mouth, but she wasn't sure about being hauled home in a car Fred Flintstone would have rejected. It was definitely past its prime . . . by about three hundred years.

Jake opened the door and put the groceries in back with the dog. "This is Spot. Spot, meet—"

"Amy Klasse." She patted Spot on the head. "One of your patients?"

"My roommate."

The dog was black, a sleek, shiny ebony without a single white or brown hair on his entire body. "I know I'm going to regret asking, but why is this animal named 'Spot'?"

"I always wanted a dog named 'Spot.'"

"Of course."

Jake turned the key in the ignition and seemed unperturbed by the loud grinding sounds emanating from the engine. "Do you have any roommates?"

"I live with a cat."

"That's it?" Jake asked, barely able to keep from grinning.

"Pardon?"

"Just a cat?" No mother, father, sister, brother, girl friend, boyfriend, maiden aunt? He'd never felt so lucky.

"Just a cat." No husband. No fiancé. No boyfriend. She wasn't sure why. Most likely it was her lifestyle. Her alarm rang at four A.M. Quick shower, fix hair, English muffin, apply beginnings of makeup, get to studio for early-morning taping. Afternoon rehearsal and promotional appearances. Supper. Early to bed—alone. And then there was—that. That physical, um, situation.

Amy sighed. She never sighed—especially not about her life. She liked her life. At least she had liked it until today, when she lost her job, ripped her skirt, made a shambles of the supermarket, and last but *not* least, entrusted herself to the care of Jacob Elliott, veterinarian extraordinaire, total stranger.

Panic rippled through her. She didn't know this man, and not only was he driving her home . . . he was invited for dinner. She couldn't believe she was doing this. Cautious Amy, the woman who avoided singles bars like the plague, had just gotten picked up in the supermarket. She took a deep breath and told herself to stay calm. It wasn't really a pickup. More like a rescue. And he had excellent recommendations from the checkout ladies.

Still, there was something unsettling about him. His appearance shouted laid-back slob, even though his eyes crackled with energy. He was just the sort of man she'd diligently ignored: devilishly attractive and impossible to categorize. He was the sort of man who'd certainly complicate a woman's life. And her life was complicated enough, she thought. "Definitely!"

Jake looked at her from the corner of his eye. "You're not going to break anything, are you?"

She crossed her arms over her chest and said, "Hmmm." It was the sort of snorting sound you might expect a bull to make before charging.

"I probably shouldn't ask such a delicate question, but who are you talking to, and why the devil are you so mad?"

"Myself, and because I've been replaced by a chicken. A seven-pound Rhode Island Red that can cluck 'The Star-Spangled Banner' and count with its stupid chicken toes."

"I don't think chickens have toes."

"Ha!" Amy said. "A lot you know."

It had been several years since Penn State veterinary school, but Jake was almost certain chickens didn't have toes. Probably not the best time to press the issue, he decided.

The engine finally caught and three loud volleys exploded from the tailpipe. Amy had never been in a car that backfired. She had always equated such mechanical indignities with human intestinal problems. She slunk into her seat, praying not to be recognized. Life could only get better. This had to be the bottom, didn't it?

Jake exhaled a long sigh of contentment. Everything was working perfectly. Life couldn't get any better. "Where to, my lady?"

"King's Park West. Wheatstone Drive."

The car chugged out of the parking lot and headed west. "About this chicken . . ."

"I'd like to feed it to my cat."

"Not many people are replaced by a chicken."

"Yeah. Lucky me."

"Just exactly what sort of job did you have?"

"Lulu the Clown. I hosted a daytime television show for preschoolers on one of the local stations. I sang a little and danced a little and told stories."

"I've seen that show. My nephew loves it." Lulu the Clown. Jake got an instant image of the lively young female clown with a bush of curly red hair and long slender legs clad in red-and-white striped stockings. He remembered her as being sensational, with an obvious affection for her Munchkin audience.

Spot slung his massive head over the back of the front seat and rested his jaw on Amy's shoulder. Amy unconsciously scratched the dog between the ears. "After college I tried teaching first grade, but my principal thought my methods were . . . unorthodox."

"Let me guess. Lulu?"

Amy grinned. "Sometimes. Sometimes I'd be Katy Kitten or a medieval princess, or Annie Oakley. I just wanted to make things more interesting. More entertaining. Time can pass very slowly for a seven-year-old who's away from his mom six hours a day."

Jake wanted to punch out that principal. In fact, Jake was ready to punch out anyone who didn't appreciate Amy.

Good Lord, he silently groaned, how could he be so besotted by someone he'd only known for ten minutes? He made a conscious effort to relax, loosening his white-knuckled grip on the wheel, easing the tension at the base of his neck.

There had been strong feelings for a few other women in his life, but nothing like this. Nothing that hit him so fast and so hard. This was scary. Four hours ago he was in surgery, happily operating on Tommy Hostrup's cat. Four hours ago he'd been contented, well adjusted, a respected member of the community . . . and now he was sweating bullets because he was afraid he was going to attack the delicious little morsel sitting next to him. If she knew what he was thinking she'd probably jump out the window.

Amy indicated that he should take a right-hand turn, and continued. "Anyway, when the school year came to a close I decided maybe I wasn't destined to teach first grade. I loved working with children, but I needed something with more personal freedom . . . more action. The idea for a TV show came to me in the middle of the night. I woke up in a sweat, thinking, holy cow, wouldn't it be great to entertain hundreds of kids at a time instead of just twenty-five! So, the next day I got dressed up in my clown suit and marched into the studio."

Amy rolled her eyes. "I still don't believe I had the nerve to do that! I read *The Little Engine That Could* to the station manager. He sat there the whole time, smoking a cigar and looking at me as if I was from outer space. I was into the second round of singing 'I'm a Little Teapot' when Gilda Szalagy, the Morning Cooker, walked in and announced she was leaving to take a job in Atlanta. They gave me her slot on a trial basis, and I've been Lulu the Clown ever since . . . until four o'clock today."

"Didn't you have a contract?"

She shook her head. "Nope. It's a mom-and-pop-type station. We just went day by day. It was always very low key. Very pleasant."

"Did they say why they were replacing you?"

"Two weeks ago Sam, the station manager, retired. The new station manager said the show needed a fresh face."

"Yeah, but a fresh beak? Hard to believe a chicken could entertain kids for a whole hour."

"The chicken comes with a trainer. I suppose she'll read the stories and sing the songs."

"And the chicken will do the dancing?"

Amy grinned. "Listen, I've seen the chicken dance—it's pretty good."

"I bet its legs aren't nearly as nice as yours."

"Thank you." It was a funny little compliment, but it made her feel better. Now that the anger was subsiding she was left with an empty sadness. It had been the injustice and the suddenness of the action that had stung her heart. She'd worked hard to entertain and educate her young audience. She felt a responsibility to those children. What would they think when she simply didn't appear tomorrow? How would they know that she loved them . . . that she hadn't willy-nilly abandoned them?

That rotten new manager hadn't even given her a chance to say good-bye. She couldn't believe he'd even been hired. Who needed to have *the* highest ratings on the air? Amy thought they'd been doing just fine. She felt a tear catch in her lower lashes. "Damn."

Jake covered her hand with his. "It's okay."

"I didn't even get a chance to say good-bye. I asked them for one more day. Just one more day, and they said *no*."

He didn't know how to comfort her. He saw the brightness in her eyes and was scared to death that she was about to burst into tears. He waited a moment. "So now what?"

"I don't know."

She had rent to pay, car payments, utility bills. Thank goodness, she had a savings account, but that wouldn't last forever.

"If I could find a temporary job to get me through the summer, I could go back to teaching school in September," she said.

Jake didn't even hesitate. "You're in luck. I could give you a job. I happen to need a receptionist." He needed a receptionist like a hole in the head, but he'd do anything to be near her. He quickly reviewed his budget and determined he'd be able to pay her a modest salary. The awkward part would be finding work for her in the small, two-man office.

Work for Jacob Elliott? Amy's heart flopped in her chest and her stomach contracted into a knot of anxiety. What an odd reaction, she thought. Why was she so panic-stricken at the thought of working for Jacob Elliott? Because Jacob Elliott was the most incredible male she'd ever met, and there were a whole bunch of warm, tingling sensations occurring in private places throughout her body. If she could tingle like this when she was depressed, what would happen in a day or two when she became her usual cheery self? Those tingles were going to get her into a mess of trouble if she wasn't careful.

She was so preoccupied with her thoughts that she almost missed her house. "There!" she gasped. "The brick Cape Cod with the tan trim."

Jake hit the brakes and made a fast turn into the driveway. He squinted at the two-foot-high grass and twelve-foot-tall hedge. Ivy crept over almost every inch of brick, snaking across windows, peeping down the chimney, slithering along drainpipes. Border shrubs had grown to gigantic proportions.

"You live here?" Jake thought the house looked like it was being eaten alive by its own greenery. The five-foot-high, six-foot-wide spreading juniper that had spread across her front stoop reminded him of Jaws.

"It's a little overgrown."

Jake bit his lip to keep from laughing. A little overgrown? She could lose a rhinocerous in that lawn.

Amy jumped from the Jeep and balanced a grocery bag on her hip. "I just moved into this house last month. I've been so busy fixing the inside that I just haven't gotten around to the yard."

She paused at the front door and skeptically surveyed her property. "To tell you the truth, I'm not sure where to begin. I've never had a yard before. And this bush . . ."

"Jaws?"

Amy giggled. "Yeah. Sometimes I worry it's going to reach out and grab me."

"Couldn't blame it."

Amy felt the keys slide through her fingers and land on the cement porch. She'd never heard anyone's voice change so quickly from casual joking to husky intimacy. His comment had been nothing more than a low murmur, deep and dusky, like fine smoky whiskey . . . or rustling sheets. She realized he was very close. His dark eyes caressed her lips, her throat . . . Holy Toledo, he was going to kiss her. Her heart frantically pounded in her chest. She took a small step backward—and fell off the small stoop into a blooming forsythia.

Jake couldn't believe his eyes. For a brief moment Amy seemed gobbled up by the yellow bush. Two slim legs frantically waved amidst the leaves and flowers and there was a flash of pink panties. He'd taken a few women by surprise, but he'd never *ever* seen the unabashed terror that Amy had displayed before leaping into the forsythia. Lord, he was a real lady killer. One smoldering look and he had her running for the hills.

He gently lifted her out of the bush and set her on her feet. Bits of yellow flower and bright green leaves stuck in her hair. The white lace blouse had a small tear in the left sleeve.

Amy fluffed out her skirt as if she were the queen of England. "I got a little nervous," she explained.

"I noticed."

"I . . . um, I thought you were going to kiss me. I always get nervous about the first kiss."

"Only the first kiss?"

"Uh, yeah."

"Good. Then let's get the damn thing over with." He pulled her to him and touched his lips to hers. The kiss deepened, and as they melted together, the world seemed to stand still. Jake released her and took a shaky breath. "Maybe we'd better go inside now."

Amy blinked at him. She'd known him for less than fifteen minutes, and here he was, kissing her senseless. She really should be mad at him, she thought, but the truth was, she hadn't done anything to discourage the kiss. In fact, she'd been looking forward to it, in a terrified, curious sort of way. She just hadn't expected the kiss to be so . . . magical.

"Earth to Amy."

"Boy, that was some kiss."

"Did you like it?"

"Yes. You're a terrific kisser." She bent to scoop up the groceries that had spilled and to hide her cheeks till the blush cooled down. Had she really just said that? "This sure has been a strange day."

She kicked the door open and ushered Jake into the cool interior. "Um, about the job offer. We certainly wouldn't want to go around kissing each other if we were working together. It would be . . . awkward."

Jake thought it would be wonderful. He couldn't imagine more ideal working conditions.

He set the grocery bags on the kitchen counter and looked around. It was nice. Light and airy. Beige wall-to-wall carpet in the living room–dining room. Creamy-colored sheers on the front windows. A big comfy-looking couch in sort of a rosy color. The walls were freshly painted eggshell white. The house had an air of cleanliness and order. It was a peaceful haven— not what he would have expected of Lulu the Clown. And it was very different from his own cramped, messy apartment. He slouched against the counter.

"You've decided to take the receptionist job?"

"It would only be temporary."

"Of course."

"And no kisses."

"Of course."

Amy didn't know whether she should trust his answers or not. He might have said "of course" but his eyes were sending a message all their own. It didn't matter. She needed the job, and she could handle Jacob Elliott. She would be friendly but professional, pleasant but firm. Everything would be fine.

Amy drained her wineglass and dumped the package of ground meat into a large Pyrex bowl. She added an egg, a small amount of grated cheese, bread crumbs, and freshly chopped parsley. She narrowed her eyes, and her upper lip curled slightly. "Now we have to be brave. We have to mush this stuff together. Are you ready?"

Jake raised an eyebrow. "What did you have in mind?"

"We gotta wump it a good one." She wrinkled her nose and plunged her fist into the mixture. "Wump." She stared glassy-eyed at her target. "Needs something. Ketchup."

Jake added a dollop of ketchup and returned to his stool in the middle of the kitchen. She was snockered—on one glass of wine. If he hadn't seen it with his own eyes he wouldn't have believed it.

The raw egg and ketchup squished between Amy's fingers. "Yuck! Lucky for you I have a strong stomach. Not everyone can mix meatballs with their bare hands," she said, plopping a lump of meatball goo in her hand. She attempted to roll it into a ball, but it stuck to her fingers and went flaccid in her palm. She looked at it in dismay and chewed on her lip. "Can't understand what's the matter. I'm always such a good meat-baller."

"Maybe we should just pop a couple of those TV dinners into the oven."

Amy held her hand up. "No need. I'll have everything under control in just a minute. More bread crumbs!" she ordered.

"Um . . . we're out of bread crumbs."

Amy paused. "Tell you the truth, I'm not hungry, anyway." She poured out more wine and leaned against the counter. Jake had four eyes. Funny she hadn't noticed that before. And he was fuzzy. She should bring that to his attention. "Jacob, you're fuzzy . . . and your mouth is crooked."

"How about we put some water on for coffee, hmm?"

"Never drink coffee. Makes me nervous." Amy placed her wineglass on the toaster. "Look, I can make my wineglass wobble on the toaster, can you do that?"

She took an unsteady step toward him and walked her fingers up the front of his shirt. "Know what? I'm drunk as a skunk. Good thing you're such a nice person. There are men who would take advantage of a situation like this."

Jake watched her fingers move from his collar to his neck. They slid along the outer rim of his ear and tangled in his hair. He felt her breasts nudge against the wall of his chest and he wasn't sure if he deserved her trusting compliment.

"That's me . . . all-around nice person." What was she doing now? Lord, she was nibbling at the base of his throat. And her hands . . . where were her hands going? "Listen, Amy, even nice people lose control. I mean, they have moments when—"

"Not me. Never lose control. Cool as a cucumber."

"Easy for you to say, but it's hard for me to be cool when you've got your hands on my backside."

Amy looked down. Sure enough, her hands had found their way into his back pockets. She must be dreaming because she'd never attacked—never even *thought* of attacking—a man in her life. "Oh. Does that bother you?"

"*Yes!*"

"Me too. Is it warm in here?"

"I thought you were cool. Never lost control."

"Never have before." Her eyes opened wide. "This could be a moment-ee-ous occasion. You know why, Jake? Because you make me tingle. That's a first. Are you going to be the first? Wanna know where I tingle?"

"I could be your first?"

"Don't you want to know about the tingles?"

"No. I want to know about the momentous occasion."

She shook her head sadly. "It's never happened."

"Wait a minute," Jake said, "don't tell me you've never—"

"Never."

"You mean, you're a—"

"Yup."

A virgin, for Pete's sake. A twenty-six-year-old virgin. He'd thought they'd gone the way of the dinosaur. Jake held her at arm's length. What the devil was he supposed to do with a drunk virgin? Not that he was in the habit of taking advantage of defenseless women—but he had plans for this particular woman. Romantic plans.

"D'ya know, some men don't like that I'm a . . . um, inexperienced person."

Jake gently tucked an errant curl behind her ear and realized, with chagrined shock, that he wasn't one of those men. It had caught him by surprise, but the more he thought about it, the better he liked it. It was refreshing to find a woman who'd decided to wait for marriage. And if Amy had decided to wait for marriage, then that was fine with him—because he'd already decided to marry her.

Suddenly, she went slack in his arms, as if some great weight had descended upon her shoulders. "Amy?"

"Wow," she said. "Wine sure makes me tired."

Jake scooped her up into his arms and grinned. The little tyke was out on her feet. "Where's your bedroom?"

She nuzzled against his shoulder. "You animal."

"That's me, Jake the Animal. Is your bedroom upstairs or downstairs?"

"Downstairs." Amy's eyes opened wide. "Are you going to . . . deflower me?"

"Not tonight."

"Darn." Amy was surprised at that. Virginity had been fine this morning. It had felt comfortable last night and last week. It was all the chicken's fault, she thought. Somehow, the chicken had made her dissatisfied with virginity. Gosh, her head felt funny.

"I think you'll feel differently in the morning," Jake said, smiling. He gently set her down on her bed and set off to find a nightie for her to change into. He opened a dresser drawer and found red silk teddies, flimsy panties, and wispy lace bras. Didn't look like virginal clothes to him. "Uh, you sure—"

"Trust me. I'm as pure as you can get." She gave him a big wink.

"So where are your sensible nightgowns?"

Amy looked at him with unfocused eyes. "Jake? I have the whirlies."

Jake shook his head. "How could you get so drunk on one glass of wine?"

"I never drink anything stronger than root beer."

"So why did you have wine tonight?"

"I wasn't thinking. You have that effect on me. I get all flustered, and then I do dopey things."

Jake felt his heart skip a beat.

"And you make me tingle. I've never tingled before. You know what? I like to tingle."

"Maybe you're hyperventilating."

"All by myself?"

Jake grinned. "Usually hyperventilating is a solitary activity."

"Well, I'm tired of solitivity actarities."

"Okay, maybe sometime when you're sober we can hyperventilate together." He selected an ivory night-shirt from her lingerie drawer. It wasn't sensible, but it wasn't totally decadent, either. Sitting on the edge of the bed, he began to carefully unbutton Amy's blouse.

"I thought you weren't going to deflower me."

"I'm not deflowering you. I'm dedressing you. I'm putting you to bed. Alone."

"Party pooper."

"Don't push me."

Jake slid her shirt off her shoulders and groaned at the sight of her in a practically transparent, filmy lace bra. This was torture. Retribution for cheating on his third-grade spelling test. Penance for running yellow lights. And there was Mary Ann Kwiatkowski. When he was in the sixth grade he'd traded a three-page book report for a peek under Mary Ann Kwiatkowski's skirt. She'd gotten a D on the report, and now God was getting him for swindling Mary Ann Kwiatkowski.

Amy grabbed the nightshirt. "I don't think it's proper to dedress someone unless she asks you to." Amy smiled. "Will you?"

He clenched his teeth. *Elliott, don't even think of it!* "Will you be okay if I leave you alone?"

"I suppose so, but, well, this has been very disappointing, Jacob. I finally decide to ask for help dedressing, and what happens? I can't find anyone to do it."

Jake smiled and closed the bedroom door. He suspected this was not an ordinary day in the life of Amy Klasse. Amy Klasse was obviously intelligent and gutsy. She had high professional and personal standards and possessed the self-discipline to maintain those standards . . . until tonight. Her self-discipline had done a definite nosedive halfway into the meatballs.

He returned to the kitchen and took time to examine the room. Like the rest of the house, it was bright but serene. A rose-and-turquoise Tiffany lamp hung over a round pine table. A deep-purple African violet in a new clay pot served as a centerpiece. The appliances looked new—as did the countertops and pine cabinets. Lulu the Clown must have commanded a decent salary. The house wasn't flashy, but it had a feel of well-chosen quality to it. Jake liked it. It was comfy.

He looked at the bowl of meatball gook and scratched his head. He should do something with it, but what? When in doubt, put it in the refrigerator. He poured himself another glass of wine and hummed happily as he slid a frozen chicken dinner into the oven. He remembered Spot and added a tray of frozen lasagna.

Chapter 2

Amy opened one eye and sniffed. A wonderful aroma was drifting into her bedroom. A food-type aroma. That was impossible. She squinted at her clock radio. Seven-thirty. She looked at the multicolored alley cat sleeping at the foot of her bed. "Motley, have you been cooking French toast?"

Motley twitched his ears and looked at her through half-closed eyes.

The ivory nightshirt lying on the floor caught Amy's attention. If the nightshirt was on the floor—then what was she sleeping in? Her bra and her skirt. A fuzzy memory of being undressed crept into her brain. It was followed by the memory of a conversation about deflowering.

"Oh no," she said. "I didn't. I couldn't have!" Motley was lounging on her white blouse. Good lord, maybe she had.

Jake knocked lightly on the bedroom door before pushing it open with his foot. "Glad to see you're awake."

Amy's mouth dropped open. There was a man in her bedroom. Jacob Elliott, to be exact. She squeezed her eyes shut and told herself this was all a bad dream. When she reopened her eyes, Jake was still there.

A jumble of emotions boiled in Amy. Disbelief, fear, disappointment, embarrassment. Last night, after only one glass of wine, she'd felt scandalously comfortable with Jake. This morning she wasn't nearly so comfortable.

"What are you doing here?"

"Making breakfast. I'm not much of a cook, but I make a mean French toast."

"Have you been here . . . long?" Amy managed, ignoring the voice inside her head screaming, *Have you been here all night?*

"Only long enough to make breakfast. I took the liberty of helping myself to your house key last night, after you passed out. I thought you might be a little under the weather this morning. I can honestly say, I've never seen anyone get so drunk, so fast, on so little."

Amy pulled the covers up to her chin and watched in dismay as he set a tray across her lap. He'd given her a glass of orange juice, a plate filled with steaming, golden slices of French toast drenched in butter and syrup, and a rose. A delicate, pale pink rose. She didn't know what to say. Not only hadn't anyone ever fixed her breakfast in bed before . . . but a rose! What had she done to deserve this? She was afraid to ask. "Um, about the rose . . ."

"I had to go to the supermarket for coffee, and I spied this rose. It's the same shade as your skirt." He grinned at the blush spreading across her face. "And your cheeks."

"This rose isn't for . . . ah, anything special? I mean we didn't . . ."

"Don't you remember?"

"I remember being unbuttoned out of my blouse."

Jake helped himself to a corner of toast. "Don't you remember anything else?"

"I remember a conversation about . . . gardening."

"You mean that stuff about flowers, deflowering?"

Amy closed her eyes. She'd hoped it had been a nightmare. She'd told an acquaintance of only two hours her most intimate secret . . . and she was almost certain she'd then proceeded to attack him. "What happened after the conversation?"

Jake sliced off another corner and fed it to Amy. "You tried to get me to go to bed with you."

"I didn't!"

"You did, but I wouldn't do it. I have my principles, you know. I didn't want you to think I was easy."

If she could die from embarrassment, Amy was sure she'd be dead in a minute. She swallowed the piece of bread in one gulp and slumped back against the headboard. "I suppose I'm relieved. I was afraid I just didn't remember it."

"It? You mean the momentous occasion?"

She detected a trace of laughter in his eyes, but his voice was low and purposefully seductive. It was a nice combination, she thought; it was playful. He was trying to ease them through an awkward morning after.

She sipped her orange juice and studied Jacob Elliott, deciding he had to have been at the head of the line when God was giving out all the good stuff. Not just physical good stuff like broad shoulders and perfect teeth. Jacob Elliott had a bunch of intangible qualities that, even in her inexperienced state, Amy knew would make him an extraordinary lover and a good friend. There was a gentleness about him, a satisfaction with life, a generous sense of humor. And he was honorable. Thank goodness.

She couldn't imagine what had gotten into her last night. She'd indulged in a glass of wine from time to time—a nip of sherry at Christmas and champagne at weddings—but it had never affected her like *that*. It probably had to do with being fired. Yes, that had to be it: She'd been vulnerable. And depressed.

She should explain to Jake. He probably thought she was a crazed sex fiend. "I don't usually do things like this," she said. "I've never picked up a veterinarian before. And I've certainly never tried to get one into my bed."

Jake nodded solicitously and tried not to smile.

Amy nervously twisted her napkin. "I can't imagine what you must think of me, but it's wrong. Honestly, I'm really very nice. In fact, most men think I'm prudish."

Damn. This wasn't coming out right, and if he didn't stop smiling she was going to rearrange his nose. "What I mean to say is that I'd never go to bed with you!" Lord, now he looked insulted! "Not that it wouldn't be . . . ah, pleasant."

"Pleasant?"

"Incredible?" Did she just say "incredible"? Was that her voice? That shamelessly husky whisper?

She waved her hand in a dismissive gesture. "It doesn't matter. I'm not interested in casual sex. I think the union between two people is very special and should be reserved for marriage. Besides, I could never, um, fool around with my employer." She looked at him speculatively. "Do I still have a job?"

"You bet. And it starts today." He glanced at his watch. "I have to get going. Mrs. Tobin is bringing her cat in at eight o'clock. Things slack off around noon. That would be a good time for you to come in to the office and meet my crew. The clinic is just around the corner from the supermarket . . . you can't miss it. Oh, and Amy . . ."

"Yes?" She gulped, afraid of what he might say next.

"Wear something casual . . . something that won't show dog hair."

Amy locked the front door behind her and skipped down two porch steps before coming to a screeching halt. There was no little red car sitting in her driveway. She thunked her fist against her forehead. "Dumb, dumb, dumb." Her car was still in the supermarket parking lot. No big deal. She could ride her bike. She hustled back into the house and changed out of her blue sundress into a pair of red shorts and a crisp white blouse. She traded her white sandals for a pair of running shoes.

Thirty minutes later she sailed into the clinic parking lot with sunburned cheeks, her blond curls damp
against her forehead. She parked her bike in the flowerbeds to the side of the door and immediately stepped
in a soft, malodorous brown mound. The four-letter
expletive she uttered fit the occasion perfectly. She
entered the empty, air-conditioned waiting room
holding her shoe as far from her nose as possible.

Jake looked up from the front desk and grinned. "You
have to be careful where you walk around a vet's office."

"Uh-huh."

He gingerly took the shoe from her. "Follow me. I'll
rinse it off for you and give you the complete tour."
He opened doors as they walked. "Four examining
rooms." He pointed out a room with microscopes and
stainless steel gizmos. "We have a good lab." They
proceeded toward the back of the clinic. "This is our
grooming and minor-surgery area . . . over there are
intensive-care cages."

He cleaned her shoe in a deep sink, sprayed it with
disinfectant, and waited while Amy laced it back onto
her foot. "Boarding kennels are through that door, and
major surgery is downstairs."

He led her into a large carpeted room with wall-
to-wall bookshelves and a huge oak desk heaped to
overflowing with stacks of manila folders, magazines,

apple cores, and a massive yellow tomcat with only one eye and half a tail.

"This is my office. Maybe you could help me get it straightened out."

The floor was littered with newspapers. Cardboard boxes held unpacked books. Phone numbers had been scribbled on the wall nearest the desk. Photos of patients were taped everywhere.

Straighten it out? Amy gasped. It would take a forklift to clear off his desk. "How much are you going to pay me?"

"It's not as bad as it looks."

"Is the cat real or stuffed?"

"That's Spike. I rescued him from the shelter. He's had a tough life. He lives here now."

"Any other animals I should know about?"

"Spot comes and goes with me; you've met him. And there's Ida."

"What's an Ida?"

"*Ida!*" a big green bird screeched from the corner. "Ida, Ida, Ida."

Amy's eyes opened wide. "My word. I didn't see it there. It blends in with the palm tree." This, Amy thought happily, was going to be fun.

Jake wanted to kiss her. It was all he could think about. Actually, that wasn't entirely true, he admitted to himself. He could think of other things, but they started with kissing. Hell, maybe one little kiss wouldn't hurt. A gentle kiss. Last time he'd kissed her he'd acted like a Neanderthal. This time he'd use restraint.

He didn't want to do anything that might jeopardize Amy's feelings for him. She was a passionate, responsive woman who'd saved a very special part of herself for twenty-six years. He didn't want to be the one to mess up her plans. He didn't want her jumping into his bed because he'd stirred up a bunch of vacationing hormones, and then when the flush of desire was sated have her wonder if she'd done the right thing.

After all, virginity wasn't something you could replace. When it was gone, it was gone for good. He wanted to make damn sure that when Amy decided to love someone, it would be the man she'd marry. And by thunder, it had better be him! he thought, thumping his fist on his desk.

Amy flinched in surprise.

Jake felt the flush rise from his shirt collar. "I got carried away."

"What on earth were you thinking? For a minute there I thought you were going to kiss me again, and then I was afraid you were going to strangle me."

"Pick one."

"No way. Is there a ladies' room here?"

Jake sighed. "Two doors around the corner. To the left." He slouched in his chair and rubbed his forehead, wondering if everyone acted this stupid when they were in love.

The front door to the clinic opened and Jake heard the unmistakable shuffle of his colleague's size-thirteen feet.

Allen Logan paused at Jake's open door. "You look like you've just been hit by a bus."

"That's about how I feel."

"The flu?"

Jake sighed. "The receptionist."

"What receptionist?"

"Our receptionist. The one standing behind you."

Logan turned around and grinned down at Amy. "Howdy."

Jake ambled over. "This is Amy Klasse. Amy, this is Allen Logan, DVM . . . my happily married partner and resident bear."

Amy smiled at Allen Logan. He did resemble a bear. A big, lumbering, gentle bear.

"Will you excuse us for a moment?" Allen said to Amy. Grabbing an arm, he pulled Jake into the lavatory and closed the door. "I like her. Nice legs, cute nose, great smile. What the hell are we going to do with a receptionist?"

"I'm going to marry her."

"Oh." Allen didn't bother to keep the laughter from his voice. "Does she know this?"

"Not exactly."

There was a knock on the door. "Jake? There's a horse out here."

The bathroom door opened and the two men stuck their heads out.

"That's not a horse," Jake explained. "That's a Great Dane. Mrs. Newfarmer must be early for her one-thirty appointment."

Amy flattened herself against the wall while the dog sniffed her shorts. "He's drooling on my shoe."

"Can't blame him," Allen Logan said wistfully.

A small, round woman appeared in the hallway. "I'm sorry, Dr. Elliott. Brutus was so anxious to see you, he pulled the leash out of my hand and took off."

"Mrs. Newfarmer, I'd like you to meet my new receptionist, Amy Klasse."

Mrs. Newfarmer shook Amy's hand. "How nice. This office needs a receptionist," she confided.

Jake and Allen looked at each other nonplussed.

"I didn't think we needed a receptionist," Allen whispered.

Jake looked at yesterday's files spread across the front desk. The telephone rang once and then plugged into the answering machine. In the past year his client list had tripled. Maybe he really did need a receptionist. He looked at Allen and shrugged. "Life is strange."

"Speaking of strange, Mr. Billings is due any minute with Daisy Mae."

Jake's eyes got round. "Did you tell him he had to have her confined?"

"I forgot."

The front door opened and a whiskered old man strode in with an enormous gray cat perched on his shoulder. Jake dived for the Dane's leash, but it was too late. The dog lunged at the cat, who catapulted itself onto Jake's chest. Brutus changed direction in midair, striving for a hunk of gray fur from the cat's tail. The cat turned around and made a quick swipe at the dog's nose. The dog gave a loud yelp and retreated to a corner, where he had an accident.

"He's just a puppy," Mrs. Newfarmer apologized. "Do you have a mop?"

Amy almost fainted at the sight of tiny pinpricks of blood oozing through Jake's shirt. "You're wounded!"

"Nothing several hundred stitches couldn't cure," Jake said.

Allen saluted his injured partner. "Dr. Disaster strikes again."

Jake began carefully unbuttoning his shirt. "I wasn't overwhelmed by *your* bravery, Allen."

"I was right behind you. I would have done something, but you were in my way."

Amy winced at the scratches on Jake's bare chest. This job is going to be a lot like teaching first grade, she thought. Wiping up puddles and administering first aid. Her experience in nursing had been mainly in the area of cut fingers and skinned knees, but she was sure she could transfer her knowledge to cat punctures.

"Poor Jake," she soothed in her most sympathetic first-grade voice. "If you come back to the lavatory, I'll clean up those mean scratches and you'll be just fine."

Jake gave Allen an eat-your-heart-out look and followed Amy into the hallway.

Amy almost fainted for the second time that day when Jake removed his shirt. He had a great body, with an enchanting thin line of hair traveling the length of his hard, flat stomach—pointing like an arrow to places she'd rather not think about right now.

She soaked a clean washcloth in warm water but stopped short of applying it to Jake's chest, suddenly overwhelmed with embarrassment. There's nothing wrong with touching a man's bare chest to administer first aid! she told herself. Lord, she was such a ninny!

The problem was, this was no ordinary chest. It was warm and gorgeous and absolutely mesmerizing, and it belonged to Jake.

Jake removed the cloth from her hand and dabbed at his scratches. "Are you okay? You look all flushed."

"It's your chest. It's, it's . . . got holes in it."

He poured antiseptic onto a cotton ball and applied it to the ragged red lines. "They really aren't so bad."

"Does this happen often?"

"Every time Daisy Mae enters this office. I keep extra shirts in my desk drawer just in case a dog shows up."

"You're kidding."

"Bottom drawer on the left-hand side."

Amy went to the office, opened the drawer and, sure enough, she found a whole stack of shirts fresh from the cleaners. She selected a blue button-down and helped him slide into it. "I suppose you have all your shots up to date . . . like tetanus and rabies and stuff."

"Worried about me?"

"Of course. I don't want to be out of a hunk . . . I mean a job."

Amy cracked her knuckles. She wanted to drop right through the floor. She was acting like a blithering idiot. Jacob Elliott in unbuttoned splendor sent her blood pressure soaring. This was probably very healthy.

She wouldn't even have to jog tonight. Her heart rate couldn't get any faster.

The front door opened and closed and opened and closed. The sounds of chattering people drifted in from the waiting room. "Boy," Amy said, "things get busy around here."

"Maybe you could sit at the front desk and do receptionist things. And you could try to find some folders for me. We have a filing system, but things don't always get put back immediately."

"I could do that. I could put things back immediately, *and* I could find folders." Anything to get away from his naked chest! Amy glanced at Jake, then practically ran to the desk.

She smiled at the roomful of people and swallowed hard at the mess in front of her. Don't panic, she told herself. One thing at a time. There must be an appointment book . . . somewhere. She stacked the folders in alphabetical order and filed them in the cabinets behind her desk. She located the elusive appointment book, unplugged the recorder, and began taking phone messages.

Allen and Jake watched in amazement from the hallway. "Son of a gun," Allen said. "Maybe we did need a receptionist."

Only an hour later, Amy was beginning to feel comfortable. She had established some semblance of order to the office, and she was surrounded by people and animals, which, she decided, was actually quite nice.

The door opened and a small boy stumbled in carrying a shaggy inert form. Tears streamed down the child's face. Blood dripped from the animal, staining the boy's shirt and jeans.

Amy had survived a cat fight and Jacob Elliott's bare chest, but she wasn't up to a bloody animal. "Merciful heavens," she whispered. She shouted *"Dr. Elliott!"* and fainted dead away.

"Amy!"

Lord, someone was yelling at her. There were bells ringing and gongs gonging, and she couldn't seem to wake up. She struggled upward, through the murk of semiconsciousness, and finally blinked her eyes open. Her first sight was Jake, white as a sheet.

"Goodness," she said, "you look terrible."

He expelled a shaky breath and shook his head. "You scared the daylights out of me. Don't you dare ever faint again."

"I fainted? I never faint."

"Yeah. And you never drink, either. *And* you never lose control."

Amy supported herself on her elbows and gave him her most withering glare. "Are you laughing at me?"

"Maybe a little. But only because you're adorable. How do you feel?"

"Totally humiliated." Adorable, huh? She was in his office, on his floor. "Did you drag me in here?"

"I carried you in. And it wasn't easy; my legs were shaking so bad I could hardly walk."

Amy watched his eyes soften as he continued to gaze at her. Color was flooding back into his cheeks. He'd been worried about her, really worried. And now he looked . . . affectionate. Not passionate. Not relieved. Just affectionate. As if some wonderful treasure had been returned to him, and he was thoroughly enjoying this moment of reunion. She was afraid to admit how happy that made her.

Suddenly she remembered. "That poor bloody animal, will it be all right?"

"It's a dog. A cockapoo puppy that was hit by a car. Allen's downstairs, preparing it for surgery. I should be down there helping him. Will you be okay now?"

"I'm fine."

Jake paused at the door. "Don't get up until you're sure you're ready."

Amy waved at him. I'm ready, she thought. Boy, am I ready. I'm ready to fall in love.

She stood up slowly and placed a wobbly hand on his desk. Falling in love wouldn't be the smartest thing to do right now. Her life was unstable, her emotions were unusually close to the surface, and besides . . . it wasn't supposed to be like this.

Falling in love was supposed to be a slow process. Falling in love came after a lot of dating. What she was experiencing here had to be lust, and some sort of romantic infatuation with the modern-day equivalent to Sir Galahad.

Jacob Elliott had rescued her. He'd assumed heroic proportions in her mind. Okay, his chest was great. That was it! The Superman syndrome. She was falling in love with a mythical Superman.

She smoothed imaginary wrinkles from her shorts. Yes, she thought, she felt much better now that she had had this little talk with herself. Everything was crystal clear in her mind. Next time Jacob Elliott entered the room, she would be able to breathe normally. She would be able to speak in complete sentences. And she was *not* going to fall, or faint . . . or anything.

Chapter 3

Amy closed her front door behind her and momentarily leaned against it, appreciating the peace and tranquillity of home. She'd survived teaching first grade and had thrived on the hectic pace of television, but she'd never encountered anything like Jacob Elliott's veterinary clinic. It was a looney bin.

After just a half day on the job, Amy had come to realize Jake never refused a patient. Consequently, he continually ran late, and his small waiting room was always packed to overflowing with howling dogs, frantic cats, and chattering humans. Actually, the humans didn't seem to mind. They swapped pet stories and read pet magazines. Only occasionally did they glance at their watches with annoyed expressions. Usually this was followed by resigned smiles and a settling of their bodies deeper into the soft leather couch.

Jake seemed oblivious to the chaos, giving each animal his full attention, looking unhurried and unruffled as he amiably moved from one examining room to the next. Clearly a man who loved his work and staunchly ignored structure and time limits.

Fortunately, Amy thought, she was good at organizing details. She'd been raised in a military household where frequent moves necessitated efficiency. Her closets and drawers were neat, her laundry done on schedule, her shopping lists were all-inclusive. She looked the stereotyped image of a dizzy blonde, but under the curls was a level head with quick intelligence, high standards, and tidy emotions. Until that chicken and Jacob Elliott had entered her life, anyway.

"I'm not myself," she explained to the empty house. "I've turned into an airhead. Ugh, how awful." She left her shoes in the small foyer and padded barefoot to the kitchen.

An hour later she had rolled out two homemade pizza crusts; covered them with a coating of spaghetti sauce, thin-sliced onions, peppers, and mushrooms; topped the pizzas with a thick layer of mozzarella cheese; and popped them into the oven. She laid a place setting on the little kitchen table, delighting in the familiar ritual of eating peacefully, and breathed a sigh of relief that her life was coming back together.

Everything about her was normal. Normal kitchen table. Normal kitchen light. Normal kitchen clock. She slouched into a chair. "Hmmm." She didn't feel normal. She felt . . . agitated. She needed exercise. The soles of her feet fairly buzzed with the need to move.

"Okay feet, now what?" Her bare feet did a little tap dance on the tile floor and led her to the discarded running shoes. Amy changed into running shorts and a T-shirt, laced up her shoes and remembered the pizza. She pulled the aromatic rounds out of the oven, set them on the counter to cool, and let her feet carry her out the front door.

Twenty minutes later she returned to find Jake sitting in her kitchen, eating her pizza. "The door was open," he explained.

"That's what Goldilocks said."

"You shouldn't go out and leave your door open. Some pervert could waltz right in."

Amy bit her lip.

Her hair was dark with sweat and plastered to her face in Betty Boop ringlets. Her shirt was soaked through, a sheen of moisture clung to her flushed face and bare arms, and her breathing was slightly labored. It was the first time Jake had ever gotten turned on by sweat.

"Been running?" he asked, making an effort not to spring out of his chair and pin her to the floor.

Amy wiped her mouth with the back of her hand. "Yeah." She took a deep cleansing breath. "I love to run. Running always relaxes me."

"Me too."

Amy looked at him in delighted surprise. "How often do you run?"

He crossed his fingers under the table. "Every day. Couldn't do without it." The truth was, he hated running. He found it incredibly boring, preferring to get his exercise in a pickup game of football or a fast sprint to the refrigerator. But the prospect of laboring alongside Amy was irresistibly appealing.

"Maybe we could run together. I don't live far from here. We could run every night after work," Jake said.

"You sure you want to run with me? I'd probably slow you down."

"I wouldn't mind slowing down some. It'd be nice to have someone to talk to, to pace myself with." Was she buying this? Jake wondered, nonchalantly dabbing at his mouth with his napkin.

Amy cut herself a slice of pizza and nibbled at the end. She ran to relax. How could she relax if Jake was matching her stride for stride . . . in shorts.

She poured out two glasses of iced tea and sat across from him at the table. You're making a big deal about nothing, she told herself. The man just wants a running partner to break up the monotony. It's a perfectly harmless offer . . . from a harmless, incredibly attractive veterinarian. No big deal. She could handle it.

Jake stared at the empty pizza pan and felt a twinge of guilt. "I'm sorry about the pizza. I couldn't help myself. I was on my way home, minding my own business, and suddenly my car was surrounded by pizza fumes. I tried to resist, but it was impossible. I guess you think I'm a weak man."

Amy looked at him sideways. "I think you're full of . . . pizza. Why are you here?"

"I came to pick up my TV dinners. I forgot to take them yesterday. The part about not being able to resist your pizza is true, though. And, well, I guess I came over to ogle you a little bit, too." Oh boy, did he just say that? "I'm sorry! I didn't mean to say that. I swear, it just popped out."

"It just popped out, eh?"

"No. Well, actually . . . yes."

Amy wasn't sure how to respond to being ogled, so she busied herself with a large bite of pizza.

"Do you mind?" Jake asked.

She might have known he wouldn't be the sort of man to let it rest. There was an evil smile twitching at the corners of his mouth. "No, I don't mind. Would you?"

"Hey, ogle away."

Amy tried to swallow the glob of pizza in her mouth, but it was difficult getting past the lump of panic in her throat. If truth were told, she wasn't good at being looked at. And being ogled by Jake was *extremely* unnerving. In fact, she suddenly had an urgent need to run around the block a few more times. Afraid that might be obvious, she opted for just draining her glass of iced tea and placing it in the dishwasher.

Jake gave her his empty glass and tweaked a blond curl. "Since I ate your pizza, I think it's only fair I supply dessert. How about an ice cream cone?"

Amy lay in bed and wriggled her toes, listening to the cicadas singing in the oak tree outside her window, signaling the beginning of another hot summer morning in Virginia. Her digital clock said 6:55. That seemed like the middle of the day after years of arising at four. A welcome luxury, Amy thought, shutting off the alarm before it rang. She missed being Lulu the Clown, but being a veterinary receptionist had some advantages. One of them was three extra hours of sleep; another was the veterinarian.

Jacob Elliott was absolutely wonderful, impressively nice, and a total enigma. He'd taken her out for an ice cream cone, stopped by the clinic to make sure the injured cockapoo puppy was recovering properly from surgery, and taken Amy home without even so much as a good-night kiss. It was practically insulting, and it was definitely disappointing. Maybe being kissed made her nervous, but that didn't mean she minded being a little nervous! Amy wrinkled her nose. Men. Who could figure?

She took a quick shower and rifled her closet for an appropriate outfit, finally settling on a peach knit shirt. She shook out her curls, applied a thin line of eyeliner, thickening mascara, and a touch of peach-toned blusher. She squinted at her reflection in the mirror, deciding she looked about fourteen. No wonder Jake hadn't kissed her last night. Criminy, she wished she had cleavage! She looked at herself more sternly. Jacob Elliott was making her crazy. She'd always been proud of her lithe, athletic body before. Now she was worried about cleavage. Yuck.

"Get a grip," she told herself. She had a cab drop her at the supermarket parking lot so she could retrieve her car and her purse. She plugged her extra key into the ignition and drove the short distance to the office.

At midafternoon Jake took a moment to watch Amy organize his office. Files were all in proper order, phone messages were neatly stacked on a special clipboard, and somehow, she was managing to schedule appointments so that he was almost on time. And, not only was she efficient, he thought, she was adorable. Her shirt was the same color as her cheeks and soft, kissable lips, and the outfit she was wearing subtly hinted at high round breasts and a slim, girlish waist.

Jake followed her startled expression as the front door burst open and a sobbing brunette dragged a kennel cage into the waiting room.

As the woman bent to peer into the mesh window of the cage, Jake was treated to a full view of her derriere, clad in skimpy pink shorts. When she straightened and rushed toward him the word that popped into his mind was *voluptuous.* She wore a matching tight pink sweater that had been unbuttoned halfway down her sternum to display barely contained, perfectly tanned breasts.

The woman grabbed Jake by the lapels of his white lab coat. "Are you Dr. Elliott?"

Jake looked into her large brown eyes, swimming in tears, and wondered at the weight of her mascaraed eyelashes. How the devil did she keep her eyes open with all that gunk on them? He looked closer, realized the lashes were fake, and smiled at her, already amused. "Yup. I'm Dr. Elliott."

"This is an emergency," she sobbed, pulling him toward the crate. "My bird is sick. There's something terribly wrong with him. He was fine this morning, and then he just keeled over. Do you suppose he could have had a heart attack?"

Jake attempted to lift the cage and was surprised at the weight. Definitely not a parakeet here, he thought. This was a *big* bird.

"Amy, do we have an examining room open?"

Amy didn't move a muscle.

"Earth to Amy," Jake said. "How about Room Three? Is Room Three empty?"

Amy knew this brunette, and she knew exactly what was in the cage. "It's the chicken," she said in a hoarse, choked whisper, feeling as though she'd been hit in the face with a pie.

Jake peered into the cage. "Oh, my—" Amy was right. It was Rhode Island Red . . . the rooster that broke Amy's heart.

The brunette took a step backward. "What's wrong? He isn't dead, is he? Oh geez, don't tell me he's dead."

He wasn't dead, but Jake didn't think he looked too good. He was hunkered down in the back of the cage with his eyes closed.

"Listen, Dr. Elliott," the brunette said, "this rooster's worth lots of money. He's a television star. Do something!"

Jake set the cage on an examining table, opened it, and gingerly lifted out the rooster. The bird was lifeless on the table.

"I have to be honest with you," Jake said. "We only treat domestic animals here. I haven't had much experience with roosters."

"Maybe it just needs vitamins. Maybe it's anemic. Can roosters get mono? He's been working awfully hard, ya' know."

After questioning her about the bird's diet and any possible trauma it may have suffered, he listened to the bird's heart. "How old is this fellow?"

The brunette shrugged. "I don't know. I bought him a couple months ago at the farmers' market."

Jake stroked the glossy sienna feathers. "Why don't you leave him here overnight. I'd like to run a few tests."

"The tests won't take too long, will they? He has to be up and dancing by Monday morning."

Jake thought they'd be lucky if the bird was still breathing by Monday morning. "We'll get started right away."

"You sure he'll be okay here?"

"I'll put him in intensive care. He'll be nice and safe. We need to keep him quiet."

She took a tissue from her purse and blew her nose. "Poor bird. All those years on a dirty old chicken farm, and just when he makes it big . . . tragedy strikes."

Jake bit his lip. This woman was going to be in deep trouble when the chicken died; the chicken had all the brains. "I'll do what I can for him."

It was six-thirty when Amy shut her computer down for the day, switched the phone over to the answering machine, and walked down the short hall, looking for Jake. She found him in intensive care, studying his patients, his thumbs hooked into his jeans pockets.

"The puppy looks good," she offered.

Jake smiled. "He's a feisty little guy. Scarfed down all his food today."

There was only one other occupant in the small room, and Amy didn't know what to say about it. The rooster looked awful. "Did anything show up on Red's tests?"

Jake shook his head no.

"You think he'll be okay?"

"Just between you and me, Amy," Jake said, his voice reflecting the helplessness he felt, "my professional opinion is that he's cock-a-doodled his last doodle."

"How awful."

Jake stared thoughtfully at the bird. "I'd like to think of him as a very old rooster that's led one hell of a life and is going out in a blaze of glory."

"It's still sad. He's kind of pretty."

"He might perk up. Maybe he's just not cut out for show biz. Hot lights and a lot of noise aren't parts of a rooster's natural environment. We'll let him have a restful night and reevaluate his condition first thing tomorrow."

Amy slumped against the wall. "Boy, I feel really crummy about this. In all honesty, there's a part of me that's still bitter about being replaced by this chicken. I'm not mad at him, really, but I wouldn't mind seeing the station have second thoughts on Monday morning."

"Maybe you should iron your clown suit tonight. Just in case."

Amy shook her head. "They made up their mind to have a new format. If it isn't the chicken, it'll be something else. Something new. Besides, there's still the star's trainer."

"That trainer looks like a real dunderhead."

"She has mega cleavage," Amy said wistfully.

Jake adjusted the IV on the puppy and closed the cage door. "I don't think cleavage is going to help her when they discover she's a lot less entertaining than her pet."

"Are you kidding me? We're talking about a station that hired a bird to host a children's show! You honestly think there's any logic to their thinking?"

She was right, Jake thought. What a shame. Amy had to keep working as his receptionist. He made a concerted effort not to look ecstatic, but wasn't totally successful.

"Well, you seem a little happier, anyway."

"Me? I guess it's because . . . I'm looking forward to our running date tonight."

"Running!" Amy thunked her forehead with her fist. "I'd completely forgotten." Running would be wonderful, just what she needed after a day like today. She smiled brightly and slung her purse over her shoulder.

"Give me ten minutes to drive home and three minutes to change," she said, heading for the door.

Jake watched Amy disappear, then glanced at the time. In approximately one hour he'd be nicely refreshed from a leisurely workout and relaxing in the cool comfort of Amy's living room. Then maybe they'd move into the kitchen for an informal supper. Then what? Hmmm. Okay!

He shook his head in disgust. "Elliott," he said, "you're a barbarian." Remember the plan about letting her make the first move? Have some patience, for crying out loud.

Actually, he figured, he probably should take her out somewhere. It *was* Friday night. He didn't want to share her, though. He wanted to spend the evening in her house, surrounded by her things, listening to her talk.

He bonked his head against the door to his office. That was so corny. He was in bad shape. Maybe he should just ask her to marry him and get it over with. Ridiculous, he thought. He'd only known her for forty-eight hours. It was too soon. He'd wait until tomorrow.

He found Ida Bird and put her in her cage for the night, opened a can of cat food for Spike, and checked all the doors to make sure they were locked. Closing the front door behind him, he jogged across the parking lot to his car, anticipating a longer run, visualizing Amy trotting beside him, panting from exhaustion and adoration while he slowed his pace to accommodate her.

Nice fantasy, he warned himself. There wasn't an ounce of fat on her, and she was wearing serious running shoes. For all he knew, she could qualify for the Boston Marathon. He slouched behind the wheel of his car and wondered if he was in trouble.

Nah, he decided, he was much bigger than her, and his legs were at least an inch longer. Of course, those glory days of high school track were more than ten years ago, a voice whispered in his head. You had a doughnut for breakfast, you eat TV dinners, and you drink beer. Then again, you live in a second-floor apartment and stairs have to count for something—don't they?

One hour later, Jake knew those stairs didn't count for anything. Amy and he had started out at a moderate pace, chatting companionably, enjoying the slight breeze that rustled in the trees. After about ten minutes of street running, Amy led them to a good-sized pond and turned onto a dirt path.

"This is my favorite part," she called over to him. "I think if we run a little faster we'll have time to do two laps before it gets dark."

Two laps? Was she kidding? He was lucky he'd made it *this* far; he was a dead man. His calves burned, his feet felt like lead, his T-shirt was soaked through, and he couldn't breathe. Don't think about it! he ordered himself. Just concentrate on the woman beside— wait, passing—you, running with long easy strides.

She wore silky black shorts that flapped intriguingly at the side vent, displaying a tantalizing sliver of upper thigh when the breeze was just right. It was enough to keep him going. Wait for the wind, he told himself. Keep putting one foot in front of the other and wait for the wind.

He was relieved when they hit a long downhill grade, then almost groaned out loud when they turned a corner and began climbing. The path stretched end-lessly in front of him, leading to what he thought looked like the Matterhorn.

Please, let the Fates allow him to get around just *once*, and he'd never eat another doughnut. More orange juice, less coffee. No beer. For the rest of his life he'd never have another beer.

Things certainly were looking up, Amy thought. She'd always enjoyed running, but this outing was spe-cial. Jake was behind her, seeing her favorite lake for the first time, and Amy imagined it through his eyes.

The setting sun flickered through holes in the tree roof, not quite strong enough to pattern the shaded path. It cast the lake in deep-hued pastels of mauve and teal, encouraging birds to roost and tree toads to commence their evening song. The ground smelled damp and fresh, sometimes surprisingly sweet with honeysuckle, sometimes pungent with fallen leaves and felled trees.

Amy ran effortlessly, relishing Jake's company, real-izing that she'd never enjoyed male companionship like this. Jake was real. She could hear him breathing, hear the steady thud of his footsteps. There was none of the artificiality of her other dates.

Even with Jeff and their brief engagement, there had always been a distance, a formality she never could break through. That relationship had burned so bright and so fast, it seemed a lifetime ago. Maybe it had been; she felt almost untouched by it. Jeff had proven himself a hollow shell.

But, Jake. Jake was the sort of man who belonged in your kitchen. She could imagine him stealing swipes of frosting from a freshly baked cake, or with his nose buried in the newspaper on a Sunday morning. The sexual attraction between them made Amy nervous, but it was exciting, too. And, somehow, Jake eventually always managed to make her relax.

She turned her head to look at him in his faded navy running shorts and gray T-shirt with cutoff sleeves. She didn't even notice the renegade root snaking across the dirt path until she tripped over it, snagging her toe.

"Yeow," she gasped, sprawling face first into a rhododendron.

Jake staggered to a halt and wiped the sweat from his eyes.

"Are you okay? You have a thing for leaping into bushes?"

"I skinned my knee."

Wow. He didn't want her to be hurt, but he wouldn't mind if she couldn't run anymore. Skinned knee, stubbed toe, minor muscle cramp.

He collapsed into the bush next to her. "Looks pretty bad."

Amy wrinkled her nose and stood. "It's just a scratch." She dusted off her legs and shorts and turned to go.

Jake grabbed her by the ankle. "Wait! You shouldn't run with your knee like that. It's bleeding. It'll swell. It'll get infected."

"Thanks, Jake, but it'll be fine, really."

He held his hand up. "I know about these things. I'm a veterinarian. There are germs in the dirt that are just waiting to jump into that cut. You need a disinfectant."

He struggled to his feet. "You need to rest, elevate your leg. I'll cut through these yards and call us a cab . . ."

Amy rolled her eyes and trotted away. One of Jake's most endearing traits was his sense of humor. Picking up the pace a little so he wouldn't get bored, Amy flushed with pleasure at the obvious concern she'd seen on Jake's face. She had the feeling she had already taken a much bigger fall—for him.

Jake was glad for the encroaching darkness as he doggedly plodded beside Amy, down Gainsborough Drive to Wheatstone, thinking his appendectomy had been less painful than this run. There was little satisfaction in Amy's declaration that she was tiring. He'd passed "tired" five miles back and was working on "near death."

He forced himself to walk up her front steps in a normal fashion, dragged himself into the foyer, and sprawled onto the living room rug. "I have a cramp," he mumbled.

Amy bent to help. "In your leg? Want me to massage it?"

Jake closed his eyes. "Mmmm."

"Which leg? Right? Left?"

"Yeah."

"You have a cramp in both legs?"

Jake flopped over onto his back. "I have a cramp in my body."

"Um, could you be more specific?"

He opened one eye. Tell me this isn't happening, he said to himself. She's asking me where I want to be massaged, and I'm too tired to tell her. "It sort of moves around."

"You need a nice hot shower."

"Yeah, you're right. I'll go home and take one."

Amy tried to keep the disappointment from her voice. She didn't want the evening to end so quickly. She didn't want Jake to leave.

"You could stay for supper. I could put a couple steaks on the grill."

Jake thought it sounded great, but he didn't have the energy to chew steak. His only chance of avoiding total humiliation was to get home before rigor mortis set in.

"I'd like to stay for supper, Amy, but I have things to do. This is the night I work out at the gym. You know, Nautilus, and stuff. Then I go for a swim . . ."

He got up carefully and slowly walked to the door, thinking that his hamstring must have shrunk two inches in the past hour. If she had this kind of stamina on the jogging path, what would she be like in bed?

Maybe he didn't want to know. He wasn't sure he could keep up with her. And he definitely wouldn't want her to find *that* out . . .

Chapter 4

Jake Elliott was a puzzle, Amy thought. He spent all that time exercising his beautiful body, and then he ate doughnuts for breakfast, skipped lunch, and ate TV dinners and fast food for supper. Amy suspected his life was in the same sort of disorder as his office, and the homemaker in her instinctively wanted to change it.

She couldn't persuade Jake to stay for steaks last night, but he couldn't escape her culinary efforts today. While he'd been busy with all that Nautilus business, she'd been busy in her kitchen.

She turned into the clinic parking lot at 8:45 and smiled at the basket on the seat next to her. Homemade biscuits and soup for lunch, heated in the office microwave. Apple pie for dessert. But her motives weren't entirely altruistic. She was taken with Jake, and the way to a man's heart was through his stomach, wasn't it? Yessir, she had something better than cleavage. She had Fannie Farmer.

Amy slung the basket over her arm, locked the car, and took one last assessment of her khaki slacks, cream-colored silk shirt, strappy bone sandals, and large gold-knot earrings. What the well-dressed veterinary receptionist wears when she wants to impress the veterinarian, she thought, giving only a cursory glance to the two police cars parked outside as she approached the open clinic door.

Jake's voice carried into the parking lot. "He's gone? I can't believe it! Nothing like this has ever happened before."

Amy peeked into the waiting room. "Who's gone?"

Jake ran his hand through his hair. "Rhode Island Red. He's disappeared. He's been rooster-napped."

"Oh my gosh. Are you sure?"

Jake made an exasperated gesture. "The bird is gone. I've gone over the whole office. He's not here."

Amy felt her skin crawl. What sort of monster would steal a sick rooster? It was hard to believe someone would do such a thing. Her attention was attracted by Spike, sitting complacently on the front desk, washing his face with his paw. "You don't suppose . . ."

Jake followed her gaze to Spike. "That Spike picked the lock and ate the bird?"

"He does look a little plumper than usual."

Jake shook his head. "No. Spike was in the parking lot when I drove up this morning. Whoever took the bird, accidentally let Spike out."

Several local cameramen and reporters entered the small waiting room. Lens caps were removed, pads were snapped open. A man motioned to Jake. "Are you the guy that lost the TV bird?"

Two minicams appeared almost simultaneously. One was from the local news, the other from a small cable station. "Is it true you've received ransom notes?"

Jake looked around him in disbelief. "How'd you guys find out about this?"

"Police report."

Suddenly all eyes were turned toward the curvaceous brunette in the doorway. "Excuse me," she said softly. "Did you want to see me about something, Dr. Elliott?"

Jake grimaced as a battery of flashes went off. "I have some bad news for you. I'm afraid your rooster has been stolen."

She blinked her thick lashes. "Stolen?"

"I can't tell you how awful I feel about this," Jake said. "As you can see, I've called the police . . ."

FOUL PLAY · 71

She looked shocked. "Police?"

A uniformed officer approached the brunette. "Has anyone contacted you about the bird? Is there anyone who might profit from his disappearance?"

Amy took a step backward and bumped into a young man with wire glasses and a narrow blade of a nose. Suddenly, astonishment registered on his face as a scarlet scald rose from his shirt collar. He stared openmouthed at Amy in silent accusation.

Jake saw the color drain from Amy's face. Her lips compressed into a tight, thin line. He moved close to her, sliding his arm around her shoulder. "Something wrong?"

"This is Brian Turner," Amy said. "The innovative station manager who purchases poultry."

Turner adjusted his glasses and glowered at Jake. "What's this woman doing here?"

Jake didn't like Turner. He didn't like the tone of his whiney voice, his shirt, or the part in his limp, dun-colored hair. Jake didn't like him because he had fired Amy. And he sure didn't like the way he had just referred to her as "this woman." In fact, Jake disliked Turner so much, if there hadn't been four police officers present, he'd have given him instant rhinoplasty.

"This woman works for me," Jake said in a tone that implied a much longer sentence. The longer sentence would have gone something like: This woman works for me, you no-taste little twit, and if you say one more word I'm going to run you right out of here.

Turner stepped backward and wheeled toward the brunette. "You're kidding! You left that rooster in the hands of Lulu the Clown!"

The brunette opened her eyes wide. "I didn't know."

Another volley of flashes went off, this time directed at Amy.

"Are you taking this down?" Turner asked the nearest cop. "Lulu the Clown had every reason to hate Rhode Island Red. She lost her job to him . . ."

The man with the minicam switched on his battery pack. The reporter from the news grinned at Amy. "Wait a minute. Let me get this straight. You were replaced by a chicken?" He turned to Jake. "And you hired Lulu the Clown to take care of him?"

A belligerent look came into Jake's eyes. "No, she was replaced by a rooster."

Brian Turner elbowed his way through the crowd. "I think this looks very suspicious. I'm not usually one to point fingers, but I want that rooster back, and I think Lulu the Clown knows where he is. I think she should be interrogated or searched, or something."

Jake reached toward Turner, accidentally jostling Amy. The food basket slipped from her hand and landed with a loud *thunk* on the floor. Amy bent to retrieve it, removing the lid to make sure her pie plate hadn't broken.

Everyone in the room stared at the clear plastic container of soup nestled next to a tray of biscuits.

Turner's face turned white. "Wait a second . . . is that . . . That's chicken soup!" he gasped. "I know chicken soup when I see it!"

Amy narrowed her eyes. "That's right. It's chicken soup. So what?"

"So, it could be *rooster* soup," Turner said.

One of the reporters made a gagging sound. The police officers looked horrified.

Amy glared at Turner. "Rooster soup? That does it! You bullied me off the set without even letting me say good-bye to my viewers, and I couldn't do anything about it, but you're not going to bully me here." She poked her finger into his chest for emphasis.

"Listen up, mister, I'm a decent human being, and I don't cook chickens that don't belong to me. And what's more—"

Turner jumped away from her. "Look at this," he shouted. "She's out of control. She's made soup out of my television star. She should be locked up. Arrested for . . . um—"

"Rustling?" someone offered with a snicker.

"How about beaking and entering?"

Jake made a great pretense of looking at his watch. "Time to do veterinary business, gentlemen," he said. "I'm afraid I'll have to ask you to leave now." Reporters and photographers made no attempt to stifle their chuckles as they packed up their equipment. The police smiled and mumbled polite good-byes. The brunette and Brian Turner remained.

Amy's eyes widened. "I got this chicken at the supermarket." She turned to Jake. "You believe me, don't you?"

Jake was having a hard time keeping his composure. His face had turned red with suppressed laughter. He nodded an assurance to Amy and stared at the toes of his shoes. He was distressed that someone had broken into his office and stolen a sick animal, but he couldn't ever remember being involved in anything so ludicrous.

Amy caught Jake's mood and felt the laughter bubbling in her own chest. They thought she'd made chicken soup of Rhode Island Red! It was an outrageous idea.

She turned to Turner and smiled brightly. "Would you like to stay for lunch?"

Turner threw her a look of disgust, then strode from the office, almost knocking the brunette over. She teetered on three-inch heels and nervously chewed on a long, bright-red fingernail. "Gee," she said, "this is awful."

Jake immediately sobered himself and went to comfort the woman. "I'm really sorry Miss . . . um." He couldn't remember her name. Veronica something.

"Veronica Bottles," she prompted.

Jake blushed and nodded. "Miss Bottles. I sincerely hope you get your rooster back."

"This was my big chance to get into television. I don't know if they'll keep me without him."

"Maybe you could get a substitute," Amy suggested. "You could go back to the farmers' market and pick out another Rhode Island Red."

Veronica seemed cheered by that thought. "Yeah," she said hopefully, "there are probably lots of dancing roosters around. And they all look alike. No one would even have to know it wasn't the original Red."

Amy and Jake exchanged glances as Veronica sashayed out the door. "She's not without charm," Jake said, grinning.

Amy punched him in the arm.

At five o'clock an embarrassed detective showed up at the clinic with a request to examine Amy's garbage. "A formality," he said. Someone had filed a complaint, and he was forced to follow through on all leads. He didn't have a warrant, and Amy didn't have to comply, he explained. He was sure the drumsticks in her garbage would be much too short to fit the description, and Amy would be exonerated.

Amy looked at Jake. Nothing was said, but the unspoken communication between them was clear. This was getting serious, he thought. This wasn't funny anymore. They actually suspected Amy.

"It's okay," Amy said to the detective. "My garbage isn't incriminating. You can paw through it to your heart's content."

Jake removed his blue veterinary smock. "Let's get this over with, now. There are only a few appointments left, and Allen can handle them."

Amy sent him a look of gratitude. She had nothing to hide, but she was frightened all the same. She'd never had anything to do with the police, never even received a traffic ticket. Now she was in the middle of a possible murder investigation.

Suddenly she realized she didn't have complete faith in the system to protect the innocent. It hurt her to think that someone had accused her of harming an animal; and, what was more, she felt victimized and sullied by the police request that she display her garbage. It lent a certain amount of credibility to the ugly charge.

Half an hour later, Amy sat at the kitchen table with her chin propped up by her hand. Jake sat in a similar position, and the detective kneeled on the floor. Two days' worth of trash had systematically been strewn onto clean newspapers. Just as they'd all known ahead of time, there had been no feathers, no sign of a butchered bird, no large rooster thighbones, only supermarket packaging.

"I'm really sorry about this," the detective said. "It was a matter of routine."

Amy helped scoop up the garbage and stuff it into a large plastic bag. "No problem. Would you like some iced tea?"

The detective declined; he washed his hands and left. The house seemed depressingly quiet. A cherrywood mantel clock ticked somberly in the living room. A bowl of fruit had been placed in the middle of the little table, and Jake stared at it as if mesmerized. Finally, he spoke. "Who do you suppose took that damn bird?"

Amy stood against the counter, her arms crossed over her chest. "You think it could have been a prank? Vandalism? Someone broke into the office and thought a rooster would be a fun thing to steal?"

"That's one possibility."

Amy raised her eyebrows. "Another possibility?"

"Who knew the bird was there?"

"A lot of people," Amy said. "Everyone who works at the clinic, everyone in the waiting room when the bird was brought in, everyone they talked to . . ."

"Okay, who knew the bird was there, and might have had a motive for taking it?"

"You aren't thinking of playing detective, are you?"

Jake looked offended. "It isn't as if I haven't any experience. I watch a lot of television. I saw *Beverly Hills Cop* three times."

She studied him for a moment. "You have any ideas?"

"I don't like Turner. Besides, he was too fast to point an accusing finger at you."

Amy agreed. "But why would he want the rooster?"

"Could be a publicity stunt. Could be the change in format isn't going as well as he'd like."

"Gee, you're pretty good at this," Amy said.

"Yeah, and I don't even have a script."

"I'm afraid to ask what comes next."

Jake looked at his watch. "Dinner comes next. We'll wait until it gets dark to do our detecting."

Amy took two potatoes and two rib steaks from the refrigerator. "We? As in you and me?"

"You know where Turner lives?"

"Oh no! Forget it. I'm not going skulking around his house. I'm in enough trouble."

She scrubbed the potatoes, punctured them, and put them in the microwave. "Besides, I don't know where he lives. And if I did know, I wouldn't tell you." .

"Hmmm," Jake said, stalking her around the kitchen table, pinning her to the counter. "There are ways of making a woman talk."

He nudged her with his knee and stared into her wary blue eyes with his laughing brown ones. "I could torture it out of you."

Amy's gaze dropped to Jake's mouth. It was smiling and very close. Close enough to kiss, if she wanted. Her hands were splayed across his chest, originally put there to push him away, but now they felt more inclined to caress than rebuke.

She moved her hands over the material of his button-down shirt, straightening his collar, touching her fingertips to the heated skin of his neck. He was nice to touch. Warm and firm. She watched his mouth soften, his lips part ever so slightly. She felt him lean into her just a bit, fitting himself into her curves.

"You don't seem like the torturing type," she said, lacing her voice with false bravado.

"Oh? What type am I?"

The loving type, she thought. She didn't mean it in the physical, sexual sense. She simply thought that he was a lovable person, and she understood why the checkout ladies had given him such an enthusiastic recommendation. His positive good humor inspired good feelings in others. She was sure his success as a veterinarian was partially due to this. With the possible exception of Mr. Billings's cat, animals immediately responded to him.

She heard his breath hitch and realized she'd drawn a line across his lower lip with the tip of her finger.

"Criminy," she said, pulling her hand away as if it had been burned. "I didn't mean to do that! Gee, I'm really sorry. I mean, you don't go around fondling your employer. It was just one of those unconscious nervous gestures . . . like cracking your knuckles or drumming your fingers."

She was going to be struck down dead for lying. It had been seduction, plain and simple, and they both knew it. And if that weren't bad enough, she'd panicked like some preteen dimwit.

Jake frowned. "Why do I still make you nervous? I thought you only got nervous on the first kiss."

"Sometimes on the second kiss," she said breathlessly, surprised at how badly she wanted that second kiss.

"I wouldn't want to be responsible for any unnecessary stress," Jake said, moving his lips lightly across hers, more of a caress than a kiss, more tantalizing than satisfying. "How about the third and fourth?"

Amy felt intoxicated by his nearness, by the prospect of more kisses. He ran his finger across her lip, just as she had done to him, and the gesture was almost unbearable in its tenderness. "Not many men get to the third or fourth," she answered honestly, watching his mouth slowly descend to hers. It was a gentle kiss, velvety soft and languorous. The kiss deepened, almost enveloping her in its dreamy intimacy.

He pulled away and watched her for a moment, enjoying the desire he found in her eyes. There was something special going on between them. They both knew it, though she was more reluctant to act on it. He suspected her personality was more cautious, tidier and more analytical than his.

He tentatively explored the curve of her spine and the angle of her hipbone with a gentle hand. The silk shirt was slick under his touch, the woman warm beneath it. He kissed her again, moving his hands along her rib cage until his thumbs rested on the underside of her breasts.

Now what? He wanted to go on. He wanted to sweep her off her feet and make passionate love to her, over and over again, until they were too exhausted to continue.

"Oh hell," he muttered.

Amy blinked at him. "Pardon?"

"Don't you have some steak to cook?"

Amy stiffened in his arms. One minute he was all lovey-dovey and then he was grumpy. "Boy, you sure are moody."

"It's my stomach. It's hungry. And I've got this chicken thing on my mind." And I'm in love, he thought. I'm trying to do the right thing, here, but it's damn frustrating.

Amy took the steaks from the counter and carried them to the grill on the back deck.

"Yeah. I guess I can understand that. I'm upset about the rooster, too. Poor thing. I hope it's okay."

It was twilight when they finally rose from the picnic table and carried their dinner remains into the kitchen. Amy made coffee and handed Jake the cookie jar. "Did the police ever figure out how the thief got into the building?"

Jake nibbled on a chocolate chip cookie. "It looked like he just came in through the front door. The police said our locks aren't especially secure. In fact, they showed me how to open them with a credit card. First thing Monday, I'm having a locksmith change all the locks. And I've hired a night attendant. This isn't going to happen again."

"Do you suppose it could have been an inside job? Someone with a key?"

Jake shook his head no. "Allen and I are the only ones with keys."

"I don't like Brian Turner, either," Amy said, "but I can't see him stealing a rooster. I can't see him getting his hands dirty with something like that."

"Maybe he didn't actually do the taking. Maybe there was someone else involved."

Amy served the coffee and took a cookie from the jar. "Who'd you have in mind? Henry Chickenhawk?"

"How about Veronica Bottles?"

"Why would she want to steal her own rooster?"

Jake shrugged. "She's dumb enough to do anything. I'm open to ideas."

"Good. Here's my idea. How about we forget this whole thing and go for a nice, relaxing five-mile run."

Jake choked on his coffee. "*No!* I mean, that'd be great, but what about justice? Your honor is at stake. And besides, I have an obligation here. I lost the bird, so I should find the bird. After all, I have a reputation to uphold." Not to mention excruciating cramps in my legs. "And I don't have any shorts with me," he added lamely.

Amy worried her lower lip. She really wasn't the dashing, daring detective type. She was early-to-bed, early-to-rise, dependable Amy who liked children and small dogs. She had no aspirations to be Wonder Woman, and she didn't think her honor was in imminent danger, but she did care about Jake's reputation as a veterinarian. Darn that chicken. He was nothing but trouble.

With a resigned sigh, Amy presented Jake with the phone book. "I suppose you're determined to do this."

Jake sent her a sheepish smile and thumbed through the alphabet. "Turner, Brian. He's on Ridge Road. Bet he lives in a condo with a Jacuzzi. Bet we find feathers on his driveway."

His eyes traveled the length of Amy. "I think it would be best if you changed your clothes. Wear something dark. Jeans and sneakers, in case we have to run."

Amy grimaced. This was going to be a disaster. They were going to get caught and arrested and sent to prison. What would she tell her mother? Who would feed her cat?

Ten minutes later they were seated in Jake's car. The engine churned, the car backfired twice. Amy suggested, for the sake of a fast and silent getaway, that they use her car.

Jake looked over at the sleek, low-slung red sports car and smiled wide. "Can I drive?"

Amy hesitated. There was something in his voice, in his eyes, in the way he leaned forward when he looked at her car. It was the way she looked at cheesecake.

"You'll be careful, won't you? It isn't paid for."

He ran his hand over the front fender. "Bet this baby can really move."

"I don't know, actually. I don't drive very fast. I bought it because it was pretty."

"Oh man! Teakwood steering wheel!"

Amy held the keys tight in her fist. "Except for the steering wheel, the whole car's fiberglass. They tell me it'll tear easily. Just crumple at the smallest bump."

Jake slid behind the wheel and worked the gearshift. "Vroom, vroom, vroom," he said.

Amy rolled her eyes and dropped the keys in his lap. She marched around to the passenger side and strapped herself in.

Jake was her employer, her friend, her partner in crime. He was something else. Boyfriend? No, boyfriend implied dating. Lover? Not yet. She didn't know what to call it, but they were definitely in deep like. There was some sort of special relationship growing between them. Relationships required trust, right?

Jake put the car in gear and slowly backed out of the driveway. Okay, nothing to worry about. She trusted him. He put his foot to the accelerator, the result snapping her head back, pressing her into the back of her seat.

"What pickup," Jake shouted, rocketing down Wheatstone Drive.

Amy clutched the dashboard. "What are you doing? This isn't a racecourse. This is a family neighborhood. There are dogs and cats and kids scurrying across this road."

A hint of scarlet spotted his cheekbones. "Sorry, I got carried away."

"Men."

Jake looked at her sideways. "What's that supposed to mean?"

"Men are always getting carried away. It must be in their DNA. Too much adrenaline. Not enough vitamin B. Too much testosterone."

"Ah hah! Now we're getting somewhere. I assume you're speaking from personal experience? You know someone with too much testosterone?" Give me his name and address, Jake silently raged. I'll neuter him.

Amy thought about it for a minute. She'd always accused Jeff of being obsessed with sex. In her mind, it had all been vastly overrated, anyway. She'd never been all that tempted to go the distance. Until Jake.

Jake had an invigorating effect on her hormones. Maybe she should reconsider her ideas about getting carried away. Now that she thought about it, she'd gotten sort of carried away when he kissed her for the first time, and she'd definitely been carried away when she was drunk. And tonight . . . she'd melted in his arms. "Son of a gun."

"Would you like to elaborate on that statement?" Jake asked.

"Nope. I don't want to touch it."

Lord, how do you tell a man he turns you into farina? Especially a man who gets hungry for steak in the middle of a clinch. No sir, you could never accuse Jake of getting carried away. He was the epitome of self-control. He was a brick. And it was really beginning to annoy her.

Amy squinted into the darkness. "Is this the way to Ridge Road?"

"This is the way to my apartment," Jake said, pulling into a parking lot. "I need some detective equipment."

Amy studied the red-brick garden apartments. Boring, she thought. Sterile. Two large brick boxes with mean little windows evenly spaced, and flat, un-inviting doorways at regular intervals. Most of the grass lawn had been trampled into rock-hard dirt.

She inwardly cringed at the thought of Jake living there.

Jake opened his front door and motioned Amy into a small foyer leading to a narrow flight of stairs. Spot bounded down to greet them.

"Spot is the reason I took this apartment," Jake explained. "It's only five minutes from the clinic, it's the only apartment building within five hundred miles that allows pets, and it backs up to a patch of woods and a pond."

He vigorously scratched the dog's ears. "Spot likes to swim." He pushed Spot up the stairs. "I've thought about getting a house of my own, but I can't seem to find the time."

Amy stood at the top of the stairs and searched for a polite word. She couldn't find any. The apartment was small and impossibly cluttered. The furniture looked comfortable but threadbare. An expensive ten-speed bike leaned against one wall. A microwave sat on an end table near the couch. Veterinary journals were stacked on the floor by the microwave. A vacuum cleaner sat in the middle of the living room rug, and a well-worn swimsuit edition of *Sports Illustrated* with a coffee-cup ring on the cover occupied a prominent place on the coffee table.

"It's a placemat," Jake said.

Amy believed him . . . almost.

Jake searched through a mound of clean, unfolded laundry, which had been dumped in an overstuffed easy chair.

"I really need more room. I need some place I can use as an office. And I could use a garage or a basement. I grew up in a small town, in a big old farmhouse. It wasn't used as a farm anymore, but we had lots of elbow room and a bunch of outbuildings."

He found a wool sweater that had shrunk to the size of doll clothes. "Guess I shouldn't have put this in the dryer," he said, throwing the garment across the room for Spot. "Go fetch," he shouted.

"I like Fairfax. The people are nice, and I like the activity, but I miss the sense of space and order I had as a kid."

Jake grinned while he pulled on a black T-shirt. "I guess this apartment is like your yard. Out of control. I'd like to fix it up, but I don't know where to begin. Your house is nice. It feels like home. It's peaceful."

Amy folded a towel. "I like it, too. I have a year's lease with an option to buy. Now that I've lost my job at the TV station, I don't know whether I'll be able to secure the mortgage."

She had a small savings account from a trust fund. She'd intended to use it as a down payment, but if she didn't get a better-paying job soon, she'd have to start dipping into the account to pay bills. She thought of the expensive red car sitting in the parking lot and pressed her lips together. Hindsight.

Jake took a pair of binoculars and a camera from the hall closet. "The professionals always take these on a stakeout. You don't always see them, because sometimes they leave them in their cars."

"Don't you need a trench coat, too?"

"It's at the cleaners."

Chapter 5

"This is an expensive town house," Amy said, checking the address Jake had written on the notecard with the address in front of her. "I guess station managers do all right for themselves."

It was a new complex of red-brick Georgian row houses, complete with underground garages and corniced entrances. Several skylights bubbled from the pitched roof and the lined edges of expensive draperies framed long casement windows. A professional arrangement of shrubberies and flowers hugged the house and the small front porch. Light glowed golden in the downstairs front room. The rest of the house was dark.

"He must be home," Jake said. "I guess that eliminates breaking and entering."

"What a shame. I had my heart set on it."

Jake cut the engine, and they sat motionless in the dark car, the silence feeling heavy in the humid Virginia air. Jake stared straight ahead into Turner's windows, one hand casually draped over the polished wood steering wheel, the other resting on the gearshift, between the black-leather bucket seats.

Amy was more intrigued with the man beside her than the town house windows. She watched his chest rise and fall, studied his calm profile, the strong column of his neck. She wondered why he was doing this. She suspected it was partly play, partly something more. Who knew? Maybe in another life he had been Robin Hood, Zorro . . . Indiana Jones.

"Now what?"

He kept staring at the house. "I don't know. I'm new at this. It's Saturday night. I was counting on him to be out."

"Why are we doing this? The police are conducting an investigation . . ."

"The police suspect *you!*" How could he tell her what that did to him. How it tore him up inside. It was so dumb! A rooster, for crying out loud. Dammit, it burned him up to have that weasel Turner pointing his nasty finger at her, and it galled him to watch her garbage get pawed through.

Man, love was the pits. It made you crazy. It was painful. Sometimes love was soft and incredibly beautiful. He couldn't tell her how he felt. She'd think he was nuts. She might be right.

Besides, there were other reasons. "Someone broke into my clinic and took a sick animal. I feel violated and outraged and disgusted. I know this is stupid, but I need to feel like I'm doing something helpful. I hate sitting around, feeling impotent and victimized."

A car pulled into the small pipestem parking lot, flashing headlights into Amy's rear window.

"Uh-oh," Jake said, "we should look busy. I'd hate to be recognized here."

He hauled Amy halfway across the gearshift and wrapped her in his arms. "I think I've just found another good reason why I'm doing this," he said, as his mouth closed over hers.

For the first moment they kept their eyes open, watching the car pull into the parking space next to them.

"Holy cow," Amy whispered, "that's Veronica Bottles."

She felt Jake's arms tighten around her, pulling her down across the seat so that she was almost under him. He kissed her again, and the reality of Jake's body pressed against hers drove out all thoughts of the brunette next to them. Amy closed her eyes and wound her arms around Jacob Elliott.

Jake knew the moment it happened . . . when they had stopped hiding and started loving. He felt it in Amy's body, the way it suddenly grew pliant, yielding under him. And he felt it in her mouth. Soft and inviting. He was lost to the feel of her under him and wanted nothing more in life than to be a part of her. He wanted to be her lover, and he wanted all the responsibilities and privileges it carried. He wanted to take care of her when she was sick, and laugh with her when she was happy, and he wanted to make her feel like a well-loved woman.

He swept his tongue into her mouth as his hand slid under her shirt. He heard her breath catch in her throat. It was a sound that brought such a rush of emotion it frightened him.

Lord, she was sweet. He wanted to taste every inch of her. He wanted to teach her the pleasures of passion. And that wasn't going to happen here, he thought, dragging himself up from the depths of his own desire.

He held Amy tight for a moment, coming to terms with his own runaway emotions. He kissed her hair and looked into her eyes, hazy with longing. "We can't do this here." His voice was tender, almost a murmur.

Amy didn't respond immediately. She was lost in her newfound sexuality, struggling to comprehend Jake's words, struggling with the knowledge that she hadn't wanted to stop. She was touched by the tenderness in his voice, and was suddenly guilty about her motives. She'd selfishly encouraged something that, deep down inside, she'd known was doomed from the outset. It was physically impossible to lose your virginity in her car. Well, maybe not impossible, but definitely difficult. She owed him an apology.

"I'm sorry."

"Are you sorry we stopped, or are you sorry we started?"

"Both. And I'm not ready to elaborate on the fact that I'm sorry we stopped."

Jake grinned at her, his smile devilish in the darkness. "I bet you're not as sorry as I am."

"Oh yeah? Just how sorry are you?"

He sighed and shifted uncomfortably in his seat. "Very, very sorry."

Amy laughed softly and pushed herself up to a sitting position. "Good heavens, what must Veronica Bottles think?"

Jake looked surprised. "Veronica Bottles! I'd forgotten all about her. What the devil is she doing visiting Turner, anyway?"

He trained the binoculars on the front window, but he couldn't see anything through the narrow slit in the draperies. "Come on, Amy, let's do some snooping. I want to see what they're up to."

Amy adjusted her clothing and got out of the car. Snooping. Great. Well, nobody could say her life was dull.

"Jake! What are you doing?" she whispered. "Get out of those bushes!"

Jake had his nose pressed against Turner's front window. "Damn, I can't see a thing. They must be in the back part of the house."

He grabbed Amy's hand and pulled her down the sidewalk, to the last house in the row. They skirted the end house and started making their way through dark yards.

"The fifth house," Jake said. "This is it."

Glass sliding doors opened to a cement patio. Gas barbecue, round wood picnic table with umbrella, red geraniums in oak casks. The downstairs rooms were dark; above them, light poured from a bay window, making checkered patterns on the black-looking grass.

"I can't see from here," Amy whispered.

"You'll be able to see perfectly when I get you up in this tree."

Amy's eyes widened. *"No."*

"Yes," Jake said, hoisting her above his head. "Grab the limb."

Amy scrambled to get a hand hold and swung her leg over the lowest branch.

"Can you see them?"

"Perfectly. They're in the kitchen. Oh, goodness," she gasped.

"What goodness? What are they doing?"

"They're kissing, and . . . um, fondling. Right in front of the window. Holy cow, this is embarrassing."

"Well, now we know how she got your job, don't we. Do you see a rooster in there?"

"No rooster," Amy whispered. "They've stopped kissing, and they're talking. Wow, he didn't like something she said. Hey, this is really getting good. He's pacing around, waving his arms. Now she's mad. Now she's crying. Now they're back to kissing. Now they're . . . Oh, geez. She just put her hand on his—"

"She put her hand on his what?" Jake whispered.

"I'm getting down, and don't you ever tell my mother I did this."

Jake caught her as she dropped out of the tree. "On his what?" he practically shouted.

"On his what do you think!" Her cheeks were burning. She put her hands to them to cool them off.

"Veronica Bottles doesn't waste much time on preliminaries."

Jake smiled and gathered Amy to him. "I'm sorry. I was hoping you'd see Red . . . not an X-rated love scene."

A light flashed on in an upstairs bedroom, and the shades were drawn. "I think they'll be busy for a while," Jake said.

He peered into the dark, ground-level windows. Nothing. He walked the length of the yard, carefully checking flowerbeds.

Amy stood behind him while he inspected the mulch around a small dogwood. "What are you doing?"

"Making sure nothing's been buried here," he said grimly. He took Amy by the hand and led her to the front of the buildings, back to the car. "I think this would be a good time to check out Veronica Bottles. We'll stop by the clinic and get her address from the files."

Amy took one last look at the town house and shivered before getting into her car. "Veronica Bottles and Brian Turner together. In bed. Yuck."

"Not a nice mental image, is it?"

"I feel like I need a shower. Geez, you should have seen them groping at each other." Amy made a face. "Not very romantic."

Jake turned onto the highway. "I suspect romance isn't an important part of their relationship."

Oh hell, he thought, watching Amy. She was comparing what she'd seen in the window to her own little groping session in the car. She stared stonily out the front window, a small frown hovering in her eyebrows, her mouth compressed.

In retrospect, their one shot at unbridled passion didn't exactly score a ten on the romance scale, Jake decided. In fact, now that he thought about it, there wasn't anything romantic about their relationship at all. He'd met her in the supermarket; she'd run him into the ground on the jogging trail; and now he'd practically jumped her bones in a cramped two-seater sports car . . . in a public parking lot. Wow. Amy deserved better than that.

Of course, he had brought her a rose that first morning. He breathed a small sigh of relief. He wasn't completely without points. He wasn't a total clod.

He took Amy's hand and squeezed it gently. "Amy, what you saw in that window doesn't have anything to do with us. People have sexual encounters for a variety of reasons."

"What was the reason for our . . . encounter?"

What was the reason? He loved her. How could he tell her that? He'd sound like an idiot. How can you

love me? she'd say. You don't know anything about me.
You don't know my birthday, my favorite color, my
ring size. How can you love me when we've never dis-
cussed politics, or gone to a hockey game, or been to a
bakery together. Maybe we have totally different tastes
in doughnuts. Jake swallowed. "Do you like Boston
creams?"

Amy blinked at him. "Um, yeah."

"There! You see, we have something in common."

"You mean, I almost lost my virginity because we
both like the same pastry?"

"Well, there's more to it than that. There's mutual
respect, and experiences shared, and emotional in-
volvement."

Amy sank deeper into her seat. "What emotion did
you have in mind? Lust?"

Jake had to admit there was a fair share of lust. "Lust
would be one of them."

"Lust," Amy repeated. "It's such an ugly word.
There's no music to it, no depth."

"You're right. Lust is out. How about passion?
Libidinous desire, sensual appetites, erotic hunger?
Personally, I like libidinous desire. There's a lot of lip
action on that one."

Amy smiled. He was teasing her, trying to lighten
her mood. Trying to weasel out of a serious discussion.

Avoiding a verbal commitment. She couldn't blame him. They'd only known each other a few days. She couldn't expect him to be in love with her . . . even though she suspected she was in love with him. "Ridiculous," she said.

"Okay. Ridiculously libidinous. How's that?"

He pulled the car into the clinic parking lot and stared dumbstruck at a squad car. "Now what?"

"Attempted break-in," the police officers told Jake. "We've got our report. We were just leaving. Good thing you have a night attendant. He really used his head."

Jake looked at the college student he'd hired. A purple bruise was forming on his forehead. "Are you all right?"

The boy touched his hand to his head and grinned sheepishly. "I thought I heard someone in the parking lot, so I came in the front room to investigate. I tried to look out the little window in the top of the door, and *wham*, the door opened and bonked me in the head. Whoever it was, they took off before I could get to them."

"Were they in a car?" Jake asked.

"I think so. That was what I heard in the parking lot. A car. But I never actually saw it."

"How long ago did this happen?"

"About a half hour ago," the boy replied. "At least they didn't get any more animals."

Jake looked puzzled. "Yeah. You did a good job. Would you like to go to the emergency room? Get that bruise looked at?"

The young man shook his head and brushed his sandy-colored hair out of his eyes. "I'm fine. I'd rather stay here. I'm studying in your office. This is a great job. I get paid for studying."

Jake looked at Amy, rifling through the files. "Did you get the address?"

"Yes. It's not far from here."

"It wasn't Turner," Jake said when they were in the car. "He was in his house when the break-in attempt occurred. I guess it could have been Veronica Bottles, but it doesn't add up. Why would she want to get into the office?" His voice rose an octave. "There's no possible reason for her to want to get into the office."

"Maybe she left something there. A clue. Maybe she returned to the scene of the crime to get rid of the evidence."

"You're starting to sound like Miss Marple. Finally getting into this detective stuff, huh?"

"Turn right at the stoplight," Amy directed. "She lives in the apartment complex at the bottom of the hill." She studied the building numbers and pointed to a parking space. "Here. I have to admit, this gets curiouser and curiouser. I never thought there'd be a second break-in."

"I almost rented an apartment here," Jake said. "They're just like mine, except they don't have a little patch of woods behind them."

"I'm surprised they'd allow her to have a rooster. Don't those things cock-a-doodle bright and early every morning?"

"Yeah," Jake said, "and I've never known a rooster that was potty trained. When we get into her apartment you should watch where you're stepping."

"When we get into her apartment? No. Not me. That's very illegal."

Jake parked and hauled Amy out of the car. "Don't worry. I know what I'm doing."

Jake found the correct door number and looked around. He took a credit card from his wallet and inserted it between the door and the jamb.

"That's against the law!" Amy said.

"Nonsense. The police taught me how to do this. They wouldn't teach me to do something illegal. It must only be illegal if you intend to steal something." The door swung open.

"Jacob Elliott! Don't you dare go into that apartment."

"I don't think it's breaking and entering, because I didn't break anything. Are you coming?" he called from the hallway. "I wouldn't stand out there with the door open if I were you. It looks suspicious."

Amy put her hand over her heart and crept into the apartment. "I'm too young to go to jail. I'm just beginning my life, for crying out loud."

Jake closed the door behind her. "If it makes you feel any better, I promise I won't let them take you away until you've . . . lived a little."

Amy gave him a black look. "You should be ashamed of yourself. A man of medicine. Isn't this against your Hippocratic oath?"

"I didn't take a Hippocratic oath. I said the pledge of allegiance under a picture of Dr. Dolittle. And he'd approve of me looking for Red."

Jake walked through the living room, dining room, bedroom, and kitchen. He looked in the closets, in the cupboards, in the refrigerator.

"This is strange. There's absolutely no sign of a rooster having lived here. No rooster food. No cage. No rooster paraphernalia of any kind. That stuff costs money. If it were me, I'd wait a while before I got rid of it. I'd make sure the rooster wasn't coming back."

"Maybe the rooster never lived here. Maybe she kept it someplace else."

"I suppose that's possible . . .."

Jake and Amy froze at the sound of a key being inserted in Veronica Bottles's front door. "Oh hell," Jake whispered, pushing Amy into the bedroom. "Under the bed!"

"It's a waterbed. There is no under."

"The closet! Get into the closet."

It was a long closet, extending three feet beyond the sliding doors. Jake dived for the deepest part of it and held Amy to him. He could feel her heart thudding against her backbone. Or was that his heart? Pull it together, he ordered himself. Don't let the panic control you.

He listened for footsteps, straining his ears because sound was muffled through the closet door. Footsteps in the living room. No conversation. She was alone. Jake realized he'd been holding his breath and let it out in a small whoosh.

Minutes ticked by, and he became more aware of the woman in his arms. They were locked together spoon fashion, with her perfect derriere pressed against his zipper. Her hair was silky and fragrant. Her breast hung soft against his thumb. He closed his eyes and silently willed himself to keep control.

Amy's eyes opened wide. Something suspiciously personal was moving against her bottom. It couldn't be . . . It was! She'd read somewhere that this sort of thing happened to men when they were nervous. "Are you nervous?" she whispered.

"No. I'm sorry. I'm ridiculously libidinous." His hands curled around her rib cage, cuddling her even closer to him. He kissed the tip of her ear and bent to kiss the sensitive spot just below the lobe.

Amy felt the heat pour through her. She'd never been a daredevil, but she had a sudden insight into the allure of the dangerous and exotic. Passion hummed in her veins. Her educated mind told her it was due to a surge of adrenaline, a primitive, primordial instinct to survive, to procreate. Her heart whispered more romantic reasons. This was Jake. Her protector, her love, her friend. It seemed natural to respond to him. It was the intensity that gave her cause for wonder.

They both stiffened as a light flashed on in the bedroom, casting a sliver of yellow under the closet door. More footsteps and suddenly the closet doors were flung open, and a perfectly tanned, naked arm reached into the closet and extracted a hanger. Clothes rustled, and the hanger returned with a dress draped over it. Veronica sighed heavily and kicked her shoes into the closet.

Amy waited, barely breathing. Hard to believe Veronica hadn't seen them, hadn't sensed their presence. They were so close to her. Amy could smell the cloying perfume of Veronica's hairspray, and a disturbing idea skittered through her brain. It was the frightening acknowledgment of things unknown, of dangers present but never perceived. Had there ever been a man in *her* closet? If it could happen to Veronica, it could happen to Amy. Tonight she'd thoroughly examine her closets, and tomorrow she'd have better locks installed on her doors.

There was the whisper of clothing being dropped to the floor. Panties? Amy instinctively closed her eyes and immediately realized it was absurd . . . she was in the back of a dark closet and couldn't see a thing. Her knees ached from standing at rigid attention as minutes elapsed.

"Thank goodness," she whispered, almost collapsing with relief when she heard the shower turn on. The next few moments were a blur. Creeping through the bedroom into the living room, the foyer, out the front door.

"I don't ever want to do this again," Amy said, standing on the sidewalk, taking deep gulps of fresh air. "I'm going to go home and pretend this never happened."

"Good idea. I just have one more eensy-teensy thing to do before we go home," Jake said. "I want to check out the Dumpster."

"Haven't we seen enough garbage for one day?"

"Afraid not. We've seen your garbage, sweet thing. Now I want to see Veronica's garbage." Jake leaned into the refuse bin. "Damn, it's dark in here. I wish I'd thought to bring a flashlight. I wish I'd . . . Oh hell!"

Amy let out a small shriek and clapped her hand over her mouth. He was in the Dumpster. She'd known it was going to happen. She could feel it in her bones. Murphy's law. If anything can go wrong . . . it will. "Are you all right?" she asked, peering over the side.

"Yeah. I'm fine, and I found what I was looking for."

"Rhode Island Red? Oh lord, don't tell me you found Red. Don't tell me they threw him away in the Dumpster."

Jake hoisted himself out and landed with a squishy thud on the blacktop. "No, I didn't find Red. I found his cage. Veronica threw Red's cage away."

A quiet feeling of dread stole across Amy's chest, and she knew Jake's instincts had been correct. "He's dead, isn't he?"

"I think Veronica knows the answer to that question."

"I'm sorry he's dead," Amy said. "He was kind of special, wasn't he?"

Jake took the car keys from his back pocket. "We're not absolutely sure that he's dead. We're just sure he's not living with Veronica. Let's go home."

Chapter 6

Amy jumped from the car as it came to a roll-ing stop in her driveway. "What was in that Dumpster? My nose will never be the same. My car will never be the same. I'll probably have to sell it."

Jake unfolded himself from the little sports car. "Are you trying to tell me I smell bad?"

"You are beyond bad. You are putrid."

"Gee, I hadn't noticed. Maybe that's why my eyes are watering. I don't suppose you'd allow me to use your shower?"

Amy unlocked her front door. "Not only will I allow you to use it—I'll insist upon it. Just pitch your clothes out into the hall. Do you want me to wash them or bury them?"

"I leave that decision up to you."

Amy decided to wash them. Twice. She stood for a minute in the laundry room, listening to the clothes agitate, feeling oddly wifely. There was a big, gorgeous naked man in her shower and a pair of navy briefs in her washer.

"I like it," she said out loud, and she wondered if she was in love. She thought she'd been in love with Jeff. What a bummer that had been. She closed her eyes, but she couldn't remember what Jeff looked like.

"Sad," she said. "Really pathetic."

Jake padded into the laundry room wearing a royal blue towel wrapped low on his hips. "What's pathetic?"

"I was thinking about this person I used to know, and I couldn't remember what he looked like."

"Was this person important to you?"

Amy straightened the boxes of detergent on the shelf above the washer. "I used to think so. I was engaged to him."

She took a long, hard look at Jake in his towel and was surprised to find she wasn't nervous. Two days ago she'd almost fainted at the sight of his chest, and now she was ogling him practically in the buff without so much as a change of heartbeat. Well, maybe there was a slight change of heartbeat, but she wasn't panic-stricken. She supposed washing men's underwear made one much more worldly.

Jake crossed his arms over his chest and leaned against the doorjamb. *Engaged.* A mysterious emotion shot through him. Jealousy? It was ridiculous, but it rankled him. He made an effort to keep his voice steady and light. "What happened?"

Amy smiled. "I used to find this story very embarrassing. Now I find it kind of funny. As you already know, I've never actually . . . um, you know."

"I know."

"It isn't as if it was planned. I didn't set out to remain a virgin all my life. I didn't even have any grandiose romantic or moral ideas about saving myself for marriage. It just never seemed right. For a while there I was afraid I had some physical defect or maybe a hormone deficiency. I mean, you'd think that by the time you were twenty-six years old you'd have gotten the urge to make mad, passionate love to some man.

"Anyway, the year I got out of college, when I was teaching first grade, I decided it was time for me to fall in love and get married. Looking back on it, I guess Jeff was smarter than I was, because after we'd been engaged for two months he gave me an ultimatum. Something to the effect that he had no intention of ever buying a suit without first trying it on."

Amy laughed at the expression on Jake's face. "Don't look so horrified. Jeff might have put it a little crudely, but he did me a favor. A marriage ceremony wouldn't have made any difference in the way I felt about Jeff. I wasn't in love with him, and I didn't want to share my body with him."

Amy made an expansive gesture with her arms. "Well, how about some lemonade?"

Jake followed her into the kitchen, enormously pleased that she'd never wanted another man, positively gloating over the fact that she wanted him. She *did* want him, didn't she? "So, why did this change from embarrassing to funny?"

"Because . . ." Amy paused with her hand on the refrigerator door. "Because . . ." She stuck her head in the refrigerator to hide the blush staining her cheeks.

Because she'd finally found the right man. Because suddenly her hormones were working overtime, and she had demanding sensations in body parts she'd previously suspected might be missing nerve endings. Because not only was she attracted to Jake, but she liked him, she enjoyed being with him, she respected him . . . she loved him. She retreated from the refrigerator with a handful of lemons.

"Just because," she said. End of discussion.

She caught a glimpse of tantalizing blue towel and busied herself with the lemons, paying strict attention to squeezing, measuring, and mixing her ingredients.

She was afraid if she didn't keep her hands busy squeezing lemons, she might squeeze something else. At the very least, she was tempted to rip his towel off. Lord, she was bad. All those years of dormant, suppressed desire were catching up with her.

"I have some gym clothes in the middle drawer of my dresser," she said breathlessly, attributing it to the exertion of making lemonade. "Maybe you can find something more comfortable to wear. I have a pair of black sweats that have always been too big for me."

Jake almost ran to the bedroom. Wearing nothing but a skimpy towel was putting a strain on his self-control. And the way she'd looked at him! He was afraid his towel would catch fire. But then she'd backed off. She'd squeezed those lemons until there was nothing left but pulp. Damned if it wasn't confusing.

He found the sweats and tugged them on, for the first time noticing the details of her bedroom. It had the same airy serenity of the living room, but there was a difference in the atmosphere.

It was warmer, more sensual. Her table lamp was reflected in the rich patina of her brass bedstead. The bed linens and quilt were peach, trimmed in satin. The room was sparsely decorated. Just the bed and a low oak dresser with a white marble top, above which a wood-trimmed oval mirror was centered on the wall. A small television sat on the dresser.

Jake stretched out on the bed and thought of the cache of undies and nighties he'd found that first night . . . satin and lace and raw silk. He was beginning to understand Amy. She kept the sensuous part of her private, wearing it under her clothes, confining it to the bedroom. She was a lady-in-waiting. The big question was, how long did she want to wait? She said she didn't necessarily care about marriage. What *did* she care about?

Amy brought Jake his lemonade and sat Indian-style on the bed, next to him. She zapped the television with the remote control, but couldn't get interested in the ten o'clock news. She had the clinic on her mind. She was beginning to share Jake's belief that Turner and Bottles knew more about the rooster's disappearance than they'd admitted to, but what about the second break-in? It didn't make any sense.

Jake sipped his drink and watched Amy. "You look like a woman with a lot on her mind."

"I can't help wondering about Red. Why would you—" She stopped in midsentence and stared open-mouthed at the television. There she was in living color, holding a container of alleged rooster soup. "Omigosh."

Jake scrambled to the edge of the bed. "We made the ten o'clock news?"

". . . and so, there you have it, folks. The question remains unanswered. Has Lulu the Clown cooked Red's goose?"

Amy felt her eyes fill with tears. "What a terrible thing to say about Lulu."

Jake pulled Amy into his arms and shut the television off.

"We must have missed something, Amy. The reason. We need to know the reason for all this. There have to be clues. We just haven't recognized them."

Amy didn't care about clues. She cared about getting kissed. She cared about getting closer to Jake. A *lot* closer.

He looked at her face, flushed with desire, and knew she wasn't going to tell him to stop tonight. Heaven knew, he didn't want to stop, but there was a meddlesome voice, whispering through the cobwebs of his mind, "Why?" He wanted to be sure it was love. This had been a strange day. He was afraid her emotions might be jumbled.

"Amy, I think we'd better stop now."

"Why?"

"Because if we don't stop soon . . . we're not going to stop at all, and you're going to get devirgined."

"So?"

"*So!* I'm not going to devirgin you when you're at an emotional low. Only a sleazeball would do a thing like that."

"You don't want me?"

"Of course I want you! Anyone can see I want you. I've completely stretched the crease out of my sweats."

"Well?"

"For Pete's sake, Amy, you don't just rush into these things. You have to get to know people." He couldn't believe he was saying any of this. The woman of his dreams was panting on the sacrificial altar.

"Besides, you have to take precautions when you do these things, and I don't have any . . . um, precautions with me. If we did it without precautions you might end up with kittens." Did he say "kittens"?

Amy laughed out loud. "I wouldn't mind having kittens. Motley needs a playmate."

Jake grinned. "Don't laugh. This is serious."

"You're right. It is serious," she said, wrapping her arms around his neck. "I've waited a long time for the right man to come along."

She looked into his soft brown eyes and wondered if he loved her. She knew he cared, but love . . . she was afraid to hope for love. It almost didn't matter. She couldn't help the way she felt about him, and if it had to be a one-sided love affair, then she would have to live with it.

Jake's heart was caught in his throat. "Are you sure I'm the right man?"

Amy tugged at the drawstring of his sweats, loosening the knot. "I'm sure. I've never felt like this before. I love you."

She loved him. He felt like his heart had just been blown up like a helium balloon. She loved him!

Amy closed her eyes. "Oh geez. I've said the wrong thing. You look like you just got punched in the stomach."

"I was surprised. I didn't think . . . I never dreamed. I mean, I'd hoped, but . . . Oh, hell." He kissed her.

"Amy, I've loved you since the first moment I saw you. When you stole my parking place. And I have a confession to make. I followed you all through the supermarket, waiting for my chance to marry you. And when I offered you a job, I didn't know I needed a receptionist."

He kissed her again. "I love you." He drew her closer, feeling fiercely possessive. "I love you."

His voice had turned bedroom sexy, deep and raspy soft. His brown eyes darkened as his hand moved over the nape of her neck. He drew a playful line along the side of her breast to her rib cage. "I'd like to spend the night with you."

"The night. Hmmm. Just exactly what are your intentions?" Amy purred.

Jake whispered a few suggestions in her ear.

Amy's eyes opened wide in anticipation. "I think at least one of those things is illegal in this state."

Jake slid off the bed. "I'm going to check on Spot and make sure things are locked up for the night."

When he returned the room was dusky, lit by two brass candlesticks Amy had placed on the dresser. She sat on one side of the bed, her legs partially curled under her. She wore a short, creamy satin shift with spaghetti straps and a dab of her best perfume at her throat. The satin clung to her breasts, perfectly outlining every detail, and molded into the dimple of her navel. She smiled at Jake's reaction: a sharp intake of breath.

The candles flickered out and Amy and Jake were intertwined in a tangle of sheets and spent passion.

"Nice," Amy said.

He thought "nice" was a little bland. He'd felt like the earth had moved. The after part, the cuddling . . . that was nice.

He grinned at her and kissed her nose. "You're going to be sore."

"Maybe, but right now I feel glorious."

Amy opened her eyes. She felt as though she'd been run over by a dumptruck. She remembered Jake and decided it was a terrific dumptruck. She had sore muscles in places she'd never known muscles existed.

She limped into the shower and stood under steaming water until her skin turned lobster red. She washed her hair, wrapped herself in a towel, brushed her teeth, and smiled at herself in the mirror. Much better. Better than better. Wonderful.

"I love being in love," she said to her mirror image. "I love Jake. I love me. I love mornings."

She quickly dressed in a pair of faded blue shorts and a gray T-shirt advertising running shoes, and padded out to the kitchen, looking for Jake. A coffee cup was on the counter; Jake couldn't be far off. She found him leaning on a lawn mower, talking to a neighbor. They were discussing lime.

Jake wrapped his arm around her and kissed her cheek affectionately. "Jerry loaned me his lawn mower, and he thinks we should lime the backyard."

Amy smiled at Jerry. Lime the backyard? Wasn't lime a color? A fruit?

"I've got some hedge clippers, too," Jerry said. "I've got everything. All you have to do is ask. I've got a daughter who baby sits. You folks have any children?"

Jake squeezed Amy. "Not yet, but we're working on it."

"Mmmm," Amy said, "we thought we'd start out with kittens and see how it goes."

By noon, the front yard looked reasonably tame. The grass was neatly cut and trimmed. Jaws had been transformed into a meek shrub, a lilac tree had been discovered hiding in the mountain laurel, and Amy had planted a small fortune in flowers.

"Pretty nice," Jake said.

"Doesn't look like the same house," Amy said.

Jake linked his arms around her. "You know, you're very sexy looking, wearing all that potting soil. And I love those little blue shorts, especially when you bend over. And is it my imagination, or have you neglected to wear a bra this morning?"

She had purposely gone braless because she'd woken up feeling expansive. Her whole world had changed, grown larger, more wondrous. She hadn't wanted to feel confined by anything as mundane as a bra. "Besides the bra thing, do I look any different? Can you tell I'm not a virgin anymore?"

"Absolutely. If I saw you walking down the street, I'd say to myself, that woman just lost her virginity. I could tell by the smile on your face."

"Oh shoot, am I still smiling?"

"Mmmm. It's very becoming." He kissed her lightly on the lips. His eyes softened and grew serious. "I love you."

She encircled his waist with her arms. "I love you, too. And it was nice of you to spend all this time helping me with my yard."

"I wanted to do something for you. Being in love is a painful experience. It's . . . obsessive. I have all this love energy."

Love energy. Amy thought it was a great phrase. She knew exactly what he meant. She had love energy, too. She wanted to make his coffee, rub his back, iron his shirts. Well, maybe ironing was going too far. She lowered her lashes flirtatiously. "I think I know a way of getting rid of some excess energy."

Three minutes later she was shamelessly naked on her rumpled sheets. She stretched luxuriously and beckoned to Jake. "This is my first matinee. Do you do anything different when you make love in the sunshine?"

He ran his hand the length of her silken leg and told her of a possible variation.

Amy closed her eyes and arched her back. "Yum," she said breathlessly.

Amy lay back in the big aluminum rowboat and let her fingertips trail in the water. Her eyes were closed; the sun was warm on her face; the waves quietly slopped against the side of the gently rocking boat. Insects buzzed in the nearby woods and a duck quacked in the distance. Life didn't get much better than this, she thought. A Sunday afternoon on Burke Lake with her lover manning the oars.

It occurred to her that she'd just gone to bed with a man she'd known less than a week. Hours and minutes, she decided, weren't an accurate measure of progress in a relationship. She could marry Jake tomorrow and feel absolutely confident in their future. Of course, Jake hadn't asked her to marry him. Only a matter of time, she told herself. The man was obviously crazy about her.

She splashed her hand in the water and knew she was being outrageously smug. It was allowed. Today was special. Every day would be special from now on.

"I'm going to plant a vegetable garden," she said. "I've always wanted a vegetable garden. They seem . . . permanent. My father was an army officer and every three years we'd pack up and move to a new base. I have great parents, and it was an interesting life, but we never had a garden."

"Where are your parents now?"

"They moved to Florida when my dad retired. I went to school at George Mason and decided I liked Northern Virginia. So here I am, and here I'll stay."

Jake pulled on the oars. "Don't have a wanderlust?"

"Nope. I've done enough wanderlusting. How about you?"

"My DNA is missing the wanderlust chromosome."

"I know," Amy said. "Instead of a wanderlust chromosome, they gave you a detective chromosome."

Jake stopped rowing. "I'm not much of a detective. I'm stumped, and the part that's really driving me nuts is that there's a clue in the office, and I can't find it."

"Why don't we just ask Veronica?"

"What would we say? Excuse me, Miss Bottles, but we'd like to know why you kidnapped your own chicken?"

"Yeah. They do it all the time on television. Then the person gets worried and does something stupid, and they get caught."

"We could count on Veronica Bottles doing something stupid," Jake said, reaching for a can of soda in the cooler between his feet. "Everything Veronica does is stupid."

Amy took a sip of his soda. "That's why this is such a good idea."

"I thought you were the one who didn't want to do any more detecting?"

"That was when I was a virgin," Amy said. "Now I'm bold."

Jake turned the boat toward the concession stand. "Okay. Let's go see what Veronica has to say."

Chapter 7

"We need to be professional about this," Amy said. "You were right. We need equipment."

Jake turned onto Ox Road and looked at Amy sideways. "Equipment?" There were gray people and there were black-and-white people, Jake thought. Gray people were middle-of-the-roaders, easing through life with a pleasant smile on their placid faces. He suspected he was pretty much gray. Amy was definitely black-and-white. She didn't do things halfway. Once she chose a project she pursued it with gleeful intensity. He'd realized that the first time they made love. The remembrance of it brought a stab of heat to his groin. "What sort of equipment did you have in mind?"

"A digital recorder, of course. I have one at home. I'll just put it in a purse, and no one will know. Then we'll have a recorded confession."

An hour later they pulled into Veronica's parking lot. Even before they cut the engine, Amy and Jake could hear the shouting in Veronica's apartment. A window flew open and a big stuffed bear came sailing out, landing face first in the grass.

"And I don't want your stupid bear!" Veronica shouted.

Brian Turner rushed out and picked up the bear. His face was florid and his lips were pressed tightly together in a bloodless slit in his face.

"That does it," he shouted back, flinging the bear into his car. "Only a heartless woman would throw Good-luck Bear out the window. You're a monster, Veronica. Do you know how to spell that?"

Veronica's face appeared in the window. "B-R-I-A-N," she replied sweetly.

"Very funny." He ducked a tennis racket and got hit in the head with a tennis shoe.

"I don't want any of your junk," Veronica told him, tossing an armful of clothes out the window into the shrubbery. "You and your big ideas, telling me I was going to be a television star. Some television star. You had me playing straight man to a chicken. Now there's no chicken, and you're telling me I'm fired. Lulu the Clown didn't have a chicken. Why do I need one?"

"Lulu the Clown had talent," Turner said.

Veronica's eyes narrowed. "You're slime, Turner. You're scum and gunk and doo-doo. You have no sensitivity, and you killed that poor chicken," she cried. "You fiend."

Amy's eyes widened at the whirring recorder. "Son of a gun," she whispered. All those hours watching crummy television shows paid off. She'd actually gotten incriminating evidence.

"Me?" Turner screamed. "I didn't kill that Frank Perdue reject. I gave him his big break, and he blew it. You're the one who killed him. Feeding him pizza and jelly doughnuts and keeping him up until all hours of the night watching David Letterman."

"He liked the stupid pet tricks." Veronica's bright-red lower lip trembled. "And I didn't kill him. What a rotten thing to say."

Turner crawled through the azaleas retrieving socks and shirts. He found a black lace garter belt and stared at it for a moment. "This is yours," he said, dangling the garter belt from one finger.

"You gave it to me," Veronica sobbed, "and I never want to see it again."

"Well, you gave me this tie." Turner pulled his tie over his head. "Take it back."

"Never. I don't want a tie that's been wrapped around your scrawny neck."

Turner stomped into the apartment with the tie clutched in his fist. "I said take the tie back!"

"No, no, no!"

There was a deathly silence. Jake and Amy exchanged anxious glances. "You don't suppose he'd hurt her?" Amy asked.

They crept to the open door and peeked inside.

"Holy cow," Amy whispered.

"You were right," Jake said. "Veronica Bottles doesn't waste time on preliminaries."

They backed away, quietly closing the door. "This probably isn't a good time to question Veronica," Jake suggested.

Amy slunk down in the passenger seat of the car. "I need a glass of lemonade."

Jake grinned, putting the car in gear and heading for Amy's house. "I've noticed squeezing lemons has a calming effect on you."

Amy pressed the stop button on her recorder. "What do you make of that conversation? They accused each other of murdering Red, and then they both denied it."

"I don't think either of them killed the bird," Jake said, disappointment obvious in his voice. "I'm having serious doubts about my theory."

Amy listened to the recording. "They might not have killed him, but they obviously think he's dead.

Notice how they accuse each other of murder rather than bird-napping."

"Uh-huh," Jake said, cruising down the street, distracted by a van parked in front of Amy's house. "Are you expecting company?"

Amy squinted at the van. "There's someone in the front seat . . . with a camera."

Jake pulled into the driveway and helped Amy from the car. The cameraman got out of the van and walked toward them. He was short and very young. His blond hair was tied back in a ponytail.

"Ron Grosse," he said, extending his hand. "I've been sent by Local News to do a follow-up interview with Lulu the Clown. This is Dan Flyn . . ." He motioned to a second man, joining them from the van. "We do a *Sixty Minutes*–type show, except it only lasts twenty minutes."

"I don't think I feel like being interviewed today," Amy said coolly. "I don't have much to say about all this."

"Aren't you the veterinarian?" Dan Flyn asked. "This is a coup. We didn't expect to find the two of you together. Are you . . . um, you know, an item?"

Jake leaned forward slightly, stopping inches from Flyn's nose. "Excuse me? An item?"

Flyn stood his ground. "There had been rumors of this being an inside job, or at least a coverup."

Jake set his jaw. "That does it. I'm going to rear-range your face."

"No," Amy shouted, grabbing Jake by the arm. "Lord, what will my neighbors think? Cameramen and vans and men fighting on my front lawn. You can't do this sort of thing in suburbia. And besides, we just cut this grass, and now you're standing on it and bending it. Shoo," she said to the twenty-minute news team. She made go-away motions with her hands. "Shoo."

She pulled Jake into the house. "Shame on you. Rearrange his face. Good grief."

Jake locked the door and closed the drapes. "I'm pretty tough, huh?"

Amy rolled her eyes and reached for the lemons.

"I was surprised you didn't give an interview. I would have thought you'd want to tell your side of the story."

"I know those two," Amy said, slicing lemons. "They aren't interested in the truth. They just want something juicy. I wouldn't dignify them with an interview."

Jake put the cooler on the kitchen counter. "We have a couple chicken salad sandwiches left. What say we eat them for supper?" He set two placemats and plates on the little kitchen table and doled out the sandwiches.

Amy took a bowl of potato salad and a container of pickled beets from the refrigerator. "I have some leftovers."

"I know this sounds strange, but you make me homesick. My mom is a great cook . . . just like you." Jake tasted the potato salad and sighed.

"This is just as good as my mom's. When I was a kid we had potato salad all summer long. And there was always cold fried chicken. I have two brothers, and I can't tell you how much chicken we went through during the month of July. My mom is a seasonal cooker. In the winter she makes homemade chocolate pudding. I'd come home from school and walk into the house and almost get knocked over by the smell of that pudding cooking."

Amy gave Jake his lemonade and sat across from him. "Sounds like you had a nice childhood."

"I guess it was average. I was always fighting with my brothers, but we really liked each other." He wolfed down his sandwich and looked enviously at Amy's.

Amy got the chicken salad from the refrigerator and made Jake another sandwich. "Did you always want to be a vet?"

"Yup. I collected baby birds that had fallen from their nests, and rabbits that cats had maimed, and rescued turtles from the middle of the road. My mom was terrific. She put up with a lot. I had fish and hamsters and lizards and never cleaned my room."

He took Amy's hand in his. "I'd like you to meet my family. My brother Nick lives in East Stroudsburg. He has a wife and two kids. My brother Billy lives in Wind Gap with his wife and three kids. And my parents are just down the street from Billy." His eyes had turned warm, and his thumb stroked across her wrist, causing her to lose interest in chicken salad.

"East Stroudsburg and Wind Gap are in Pennsylvania?" she asked halfheartedly, trying to steel herself against the rush of heat in her body.

He nibbled her fingertips, closed his eyes and pressed a kiss into the palm of her hand. "Mmmm. Pennsylvania." His voice hummed against her skin.

"Pennsylvania is very romantic. In the Poconos they have honeymoon hotels with heart-shaped bathtubs. And the northwestern part of the state is wilderness with deer and bear and raccoons."

"Raccoons," Amy mechanically repeated, watching him kiss her wrist and work his way up her arm.

He skirted the table and pulled her to him. "You make me crazy," he rumbled in her ear. "I can't even sit across from you at the kitchen table. I keep thinking about you in bed, naked."

Amy shivered. She liked the easy possessiveness of Jake's touch.

They walked hand in hand to the bedroom and kissed again. Amy turned to close the curtains and gasped in dismay. "They're still here!"

Jake looked out the window. The van was parked across the street. "What are they doing there?"

Amy gritted her teeth. "They're waiting for a story. Ugly little scandalmongers."

"I don't believe this. This is all over a chicken. The bird wasn't even healthy."

Amy made a rude gesture and snapped the curtains closed. "Damn."

Jake tweaked a blond curl. "Boy, you're really steamed."

"These guys could make life very unpleasant. They'll stick to me like glue until they get something damaging, or until a better story comes along. I'm Lulu the Clown. There are lots of children out there in television land who love and respect me. I have a responsibility to those kids. It was bad enough they blipped me off the air without so much as an explanation, but now my personal conduct is under attack."

He kissed her nose affectionately. "This is a painful question to ask, but I should go home now, shouldn't I?"

"Yes. I can't afford to have you spend the night here." She touched his lower lip with her fingertip. "I don't want you to go."

Jake smiled. "I know. Don't worry. I'll be back."

Amy waved good-bye to Jake and locked all her doors. She drew her curtains closed, took the iron poker from the fireplace, and checked each and every closet. What a goose, she thought. How many years had she lived alone . . . and now suddenly she was frightened. Not so much frightened as uneasy. The house didn't feel right. It was empty. It needed Jake.

Jake sank deep into his couch, his long legs stretched in front of him, crossed at the ankles. Spot grunted and flopped down under the coffee table. "Look at this place, Spot. It's a dump."

Just two weeks ago he'd thought it was a palace. He'd arranged everything around his favorite couch cushion. The TV, the microwave, and his veterinary journals were all within arm's reach. He never had trouble finding clothes because they were spread across the floor. He'd lived like this for as long as he could remember. Weeks. Maybe years. Now all of a sudden he didn't like it. It was the messy habitat of a couch potato.

How had he become such a lazy slob? Practice, he decided. Years and years of practice had honed his slobbery to a fine art. Not only was his home a mess, but his body was falling apart. Amy had almost killed him on the jogging trail.

He looked at his watch. Eight o'clock. Not too late. He carried the microwave to the kitchen and found a place for it on the counter.

"Look at this counter," he said to Spot. "Immaculate. You know why? Because I never use it."

He shook his head in silent rebuke as he examined his refrigerator. A can of coffee and a six-pack of beer. Two TV dinners resided in his freezer.

A wave of lonely depression washed over him. Amy's refrigerator had all sorts of good things in it, and her kitchen smelled like cookies and daffodils. Jake wrinkled his nose. His kitchen smelled like Spot.

An hour later Jake straggled into his apartment with bags of groceries. He filled his refrigerator with milk and cheese and a container of potato salad. He artfully arranged his apples and oranges and grapefruits. He proudly stuffed a chicken into the meat drawer, enormously pleased with his purchase, despite the fact that he hadn't a clue what to do with it.

"Only healthy food," he said to Spot. "No more greasy chips."

Spot looked disappointed. He sniffed at a bag of carrots and went back to the couch.

"And that's not all. We're going running." He clinked the leash onto the dog's collar and pranced around the room.

"Come on, Spot, wake up those muscles. Get the lead out. Let's go pound some pavement."

Jake's T-shirt was soaked through when he returned to his apartment. He unlocked the door and leaned against it for a minute, catching his breath, watching Spot bound up the stairs. "Show-off," Jake grumbled.

He labored up the stairs and went straight to the kitchen for a glass of orange juice. "This is so damn healthy," he said, leaning against the counter. "Why isn't it any fun? How come everything that's fun contributes to heart disease?" And why am I feeling so grouchy? he thought. He'd moved his microwave, bought good food, and run his buns off. He kicked at the kitchen chair and muttered an oath. He wanted to be with Amy.

There was more to a refrigerator than apples and oranges. He couldn't simulate her kitchen any more than he could pretend she was in his bed. He'd changed, he realized. A whole chapter of his life had ended. His carefree bachelor days were gone.

Good riddance, he thought. He was never much of a bachelor, anyway. He wanted to be married. He wanted mortgage payments and crabgrass and Amy snuggled next to him for the rest of his life. Amy, who felt responsible to a bunch of Munchkins.

He stretched on his bed and linked his hands behind his head, wondering what Amy was doing. He didn't like those two slimeballs camped outside her house, but he felt powerless to remove them. He picked up the phone to call her and realized he didn't know her number. He tried information, but she wasn't listed.

"That's it. I'm going over there."

He stopped at the head of the stairs. He couldn't go. It would compromise Amy's image. "But maybe she's in danger. Maybe those creeps are knocking on her door right now." Jake, he told himself, this is the woman who wasted Safeway. Probably he should worry about the creeps. "Okay," he shouted, making flamboyant gestures, "I'm going to take a shower. I'm going to put this out of my mind. I'm being silly, right?"

He was still asking that question at five in the morning. He was freshly showered and dressed for the office in a button-down and striped tie. He'd eaten a grapefruit, drunk a gallon of coffee, and tried to fry an egg, but it had stuck to the nonstick pan.

"So I'm being silly. Big deal. You know what they say. Better silly than sorry. I'm just going to go over there and check things out. I'll be cool. No one will know."

It was black as pitch when Jake drove past Amy's house in a camouflaging cloud of his own exhaust. The van was still parked across the street, and the little Cape Cod house was ominously dark. Jake swore softly and continued on.

He parked around the corner and crept through a neighboring yard. He climbed Amy's split-rail fence and sprinted across her back lawn. Now what? He tried windows. If he found any of them open, he was going to throttle her. Okay, all windows secure. Patio door locked with jimmy bar. He tiptoed up the stairs to her deck. Deck door locked with jimmy bar. Good. Motley looked at him from the other side of the sliding door and meowed. Jake tapped on the window to the cat.

"Kitty, kitty, kitty," he said. Motley continued to howl. Jake saw a light flash on in the hall and a dark figure shuffle out of the shadows.

Amy scratched her head with both hands, yawned, and stretched. "Motley, you're going to wake up the whole neighborhood. How can anybody sleep with this racket going . . . *Ehhhhhh!*" she screamed. There was someone on her porch! He was awful. Huge and crazy looking and . . . It was Jake.

She slumped against the wall and put her hand over her heart. "It's the big one," she said. "Heart attack city." She opened the sliding door and pulled Jake inside. "What the devil are you doing out there? You scared me half to death."

"I . . . um, I came for breakfast. I tried to make an egg, but it stuck to the pan."

Amy cocked an eye at him. "Breakfast? Are you kidding me?"

"Okay, so I was worried. And lonely." He stuffed his hands into his pockets and grinned his most endearing grin. "And hungry."

Hungry she could believe. He was looking at her as if she were the last jelly doughnut in the world. "Jake, the sun will be coming up in half an hour. How are you going to get out of here?"

"Simple. Once you leave, they'll leave. Then I leave."

"And you want to waste time having breakfast?"

Jake removed his tie and followed her into the bedroom. What a strumpet, he thought happily. She wore a pale-pink-satin shirt-type nightgown that was rolled at the elbow and slit up the side with matching panties under the shirt. The sort with wide flared legs, like shorts. The sort you could reach your hand into with no trouble at all. The sort you'd strain your eyeballs trying to get a peek into.

He quickly stripped and slid between sheets that were still warm from her body and subtly fragrant with perfume and shampoo. Amy straddled him, resting her silky bottom on his thighs. She slowly unbuttoned her shirt, letting it hang loose while she leaned forward to kiss him. He reached for her and she retreated, laughing.

"Tease," he said huskily.

"You ain't seen nothing, yet."

They lay together for a long time afterward in silent affection. Amy was the first to speak. "I'm going to be late for work," she said softly.

"Maybe your boss will give you the day off."

She sat up and stretched luxuriously. "I don't think so. He's a terrible slavedriver. Work, work, work."

Jake slapped at her bare bottom, but missed, as she headed for the shower. "Do I get to share a shower with you?"

"Definitely not. I know about your showers. You can use the upstairs bathroom." She washed quickly, towel-dried her hair, and shook her head to fluff her curls. She decided on black cotton slacks and a bright yellow knit shirt, dusted a hint of blush on her cheekbones, and swiped at her eyelashes with the mascara wand.

"Perfect," she said to her reflection in the bedroom mirror. "The guys in the van couldn't possibly miss this shirt."

She had coffee brewed and an omelet browned to perfection when Jake entered the kitchen. They sat opposite each other at the little table.

Jake cleared his throat and tapped his fork on his coffee mug to the tune of "Yankee Doodle." He'd reached a decision while he was in the shower. He was going to ask her to marry him. He couldn't manage another sleepless night. Besides, they'd known each other for five days. That seemed like a respectable amount of time. It wasn't as if they were rushing into anything.

"Amy," he began.

Amy looked at him over the rim of her teacup.

"Amy . . ." He wondered if a breakfast table was romantic enough. He wanted to do this right. After all, proposing to a woman wasn't an everyday occurrence. Someday they would be telling their children about this. He could just hear it. Amy would lower her voice conspiratorially and say to their daughter, ". . . it was so romantic. Your father swept me off my feet at the breakfast table."

Jake added salt to his coffee and stirred it with his fork.

Amy's eyes widened as she watched this. Premature dementia, she thought. Probably brought on by too much sex. Maybe his tie was too tight, cutting off the oxygen to his brain.

He leaned forward and took her hand. "Amy . . ." Lord, what if she turned him down? It was possible. She was a goddess, and he was just an out-of-shape veterinarian who lost chickens. He didn't even have a decent car. Probably he was going bald and no one had told him. Baldness was one of those things everyone knew but the baldee, because it crept up on you from behind, starting with a small shiny patch of skin on the top of your head. And he thought he detected the beginnings of a paunch this morning. He shook his head sadly. She'd never marry him. Never in a million years. "Amy . . ."

"*Yes?*" Amy shouted.

Jake stared at her for a moment, then let out a whoosh of breath. "I was afraid you'd say no."

Amy blinked at him. "I don't think I heard the question."

"Didn't I ask you to marry me?"

"Was that what you were trying to do?" Amy said, trying to suppress the laughter.

"Did I do it all right? Was it romantic enough?"

Amy nodded. "It was wonderful. I was just distracted for a moment because your tie is hanging in your coffee."

Jake looked down, a horrified expression registering in his eyes.

Amy gently lifted the tie and blotted the tip with a paper towel. How could she not love a man who proposed with his tie floating in his coffee? It was . . . real.

Chapter 8

The twenty-minute men had followed Amy, just as Jake had predicted. She could see them through the window in the clinic waiting room. They were sitting in their van, drinking soda, doing crossword puzzles. Creepy, Amy thought. She was living in a goldfish bowl. She had weasely little men following her around, waiting for her to say the wrong thing, waiting for her to make the wrong move. A shiver ran down her spine. Definitely creepy.

She watched Jake come chugging into the lot and breathed a sigh of relief. Jake, the trusty dispeller of gloom and doom. The knight of the breakfast table. Slayer of dragons and rude newsmen.

Her hero coasted to a stop beside the van. His maroon jeep-thing shuddered violently, backfired, and settled down to a brooding, sullen silence.

Mrs. Boyd jumped from her seat in the waiting area. "What was that? Was that a gunshot?"

Amy sent her a crooked smile. "That was Dr. Elliott. His car backfired."

"Oh yes," Mrs. Boyd said. "I'd forgotten about his car."

Jake came whistling into the office with Spot in tow, a new tie dangling from the collar of his button-down shirt and the morning paper under his arm.

"Good morning," he said to Mrs. Boyd and her cat, Sarah. "Good morning, Amy," he said, plopping the paper on her desk and planting a big smackeroo kiss on her surprised lips.

"We're engaged," he explained to Mrs. Boyd. "We're getting married soon. Maybe this afternoon, if we get a cancellation."

Mrs. Boyd smiled her approval.

"Do we have any cancellations?" Jake asked Amy.

Amy wasn't able to share his enthusiasm. An uneasy feeling was prickling at the nape of her neck, and there was a leaden depression settling in the pit of her stomach.

"We've had four cancellations," she whispered, turning her back to Mrs. Boyd. "All from people who were bringing their animals in for surgery that would require boarding."

Jake raised his eyebrows in question.

"One woman asked if we'd seen the morning paper. She sounded sort of . . . huffy."

Jake unfolded the paper on Amy's desk and began turning pages. "Omigod."

Mrs. Boyd looked up with interest.

Amy read the headline and clapped her hand to her mouth.

"Is that the article about the clinic?" Mrs. Boyd asked. "Isn't that a clever headline?"

"Clever," Jake said numbly. He read it aloud. "Doc Loses Cock." It sounded as if he'd been emasculated. The story itself was innocuous enough. More human interest and humor than criminal, but obviously it was damaging. Nine o'clock in the morning and they'd had four cancellations.

"This is crazy," he said to Amy. "This calls for drastic action."

Amy nervously twisted a pencil in her hand. "What did you have in mind?"

"Jelly doughnuts."

"Pardon?"

"There's a great bakery in the supermarket across the street." He reached into his pocket and handed Amy a twenty-dollar bill. "Some men smoke. Some men drink. I eat jelly doughnuts. I always feel better after a jelly doughnut. Get some for yourself, too. And don't forget Mrs. Boyd."

"I like the kind with cinnamon sugar," Mrs. Boyd said.

Amy trudged over to the bakery. This was all her fault. Jake had turned to jelly doughnuts because of her. What would be next? Boston creams? Another week of this and he'd be hooked on Napoleons and éclairs.

She pushed through the bakery door and took a number. This chicken stuff was only newsworthy because Lulu was implicated, she thought bitterly. She'd been hardly noticed as a clown, important to just a few hundred children, but as a chicken thief she was infamous, a scandalous joke. If it continued she'd ruin Jake's business. People didn't want to leave their beloved pets in the hands of a woman accused of eating her competition for lunch.

She stepped up to the counter and chose a dozen doughnuts. Why couldn't she have gotten a job in a bakery? Bakeries were cozy and smelled great, and if you were accused of cannibalizing the doughnuts nobody cared too much.

The girl behind the counter stared at Amy. "Do I know you?"

Amy shook her head vigorously. "Nope. I'm new in town . . ."

"I know! You're Lulu. Your picture's in the paper." She handed Amy the bag of doughnuts and winked. "Having a change of menu today, huh?"

By midafternoon Amy had covered her bright yellow sweater with a blue lab coat, hoping to be less conspicuous. Most of the clients had stared at their toes or buried themselves in magazines. A few had good-naturedly flapped their wings and clucked at her. One woman asked for her autograph.

At five o'clock Amy had a splitting headache and was almost happy when the last two appointments of the day canceled. She wanted to go home and hide. She wasn't usually one to run from a problem, but this wasn't the sort of thing she could easily confront. If she said nothing at all, it implied guilt. And if she tried to explain, it smacked of guilt.

Jake perched on the corner of her desk, a stethoscope dangling from his neck. "Why so glum?"

"Never in a million years did I think it would come to this. People actually believe I took that bird."

Jake made a face. "Nah. They're just confused. Once they have the time to sort it out, everything will be fine. In a week this whole thing will have been forgotten, and we'll be sitting around having a good laugh out of it."

"I think you're being optimistic."

"You bet," Jake said, hopping off her desk. "This is a special day for me. I got engaged today, and I'm taking my wife-to-be out to a fancy restaurant to celebrate."

"I don't think that's such a good idea. Maybe we should keep a low profile for a while . . ."

Jake pulled her to her feet. "We'll be discreet. I'll wear my glasses with the nose attached, and no one will recognize us. You go home and get all dressed up in something pretty. I'll pick you up at seven."

She wondered if Jake was right. Would it all go away in a week? What if it didn't? Everything he'd worked for would be ruined. She turned onto Ox Road, solemnly noting the twenty-minute men close behind. They must be getting tired. Didn't they need a shower? Why didn't they just go out and get a respectable job like everybody else . . . selling shoes or shampooing carpets. She parked in her driveway, and the newsmen parked half a block away.

"How subtle," she said, sarcastically rolling her eyes.

Not even a bubble bath could wash away the feeling of foreboding. She should be ecstatically happy, she thought. She was in love, and she was engaged. Her lawn had gotten cut. What more could a woman want? She lethargically soaped a leg and realized the water had gotten cold. Hormones, she thought, pulling the plug. It had to be hormones that made her so droopy. She'd used up all her hormones this morning and now she was empty.

She dropped a pale-pink dress over her head and felt a little better. It was her favorite dress. Romantic feeling and romantic looking, with a softly flared skirt, a clingy bodice, low scoop neck, and slightly ruffled cap sleeves. She slipped her feet into strappy bone sandals and finished the outfit with a pair of antique pearl earrings.

"Very nice," Jake said when he saw her. His eyes said more. They were liquid and admiring, filled with pride and infinite love for the woman standing before him. He was almost overwhelmed with a feeling of fiercely possessive tenderness. She seemed so delicate and vulnerable in the simple little dress that subtly molded to her body.

Jake locked the front door and waved to the van. "We're going out to dinner," he shouted. "Hope you've got a tie!" He turned to Amy. "Don't they ever give up?"

Amy shook her head. "I suppose you have to admire their tenacity, if not their judgment. What I can't understand is, why me? There must be a real news void in Fairfax County."

Jake gunned the motor of the sporty red car. "Sorry," he said. "I'm not used to a car that starts the first time."

He backed out of the driveway and reached for Amy's hand as he slowly drove through her neighborhood.

It was a stable, family-oriented subdivision that took pride in its appearance. Lots were large, having been carved at a time when land was readily available. Trees planted by those first homeowners, some twenty years previously, were mature and plentiful. Lawns and shrubbery were lush from spring rains and an unseasonably warm May. Flowers grew everywhere. Huge thick beds of impatiens nestled in red-and-white glory at the base of azalea bushes, dwarf hollies, and juniper. Clematis vined over mailboxes, geraniums grew in oak tubs on porches, and lavender phlox marched along sidewalks.

A good place to raise children, Jake thought. Good schools, good people. He could easily afford to buy the Cape Cod, and with three bedrooms and bath upstairs, it was large enough for a whole passel of kids. He wondered about Amy's views on having a family. Maybe she wanted a career. That was okay. Whatever Amy wanted. If they couldn't have kids, they'd raise dogs.

Amy felt contentment creeping into her. It radiated from Jake's hand, up her arm to her heart. He was smiling, thinking secret thoughts, and he generated peace and well-being. She was an alarmist, she decided. A few cancellations didn't mean the end of the world. She should listen to Jake. Everything would be fine. It was all absurd, anyway. Wasn't it?

Jake's hand tightened on hers. "What is it, Amy? What are you thinking? First, you're tense, then you relax, then you're tense. Are you having second thoughts about marrying me?"

"Remember I told you my dad was in the service? Well, when I was a kid, we were always moving. It seemed like I was constantly struggling to prove myself. I had to prove I was smart to new teachers. I had to prove I was trustworthy to new friends. Every time I reached that spot where things started to come together, we'd move. I developed a kind of sense about it, like an animal that can feel earth tremors before they're recorded on a seismograph. I'd get an uneasy feeling in the pit of my stomach, and sure enough, my dad would come home and announce his new orders. I keep getting that feeling, Jake. Little tremors. I can't get rid of them."

He didn't know what to say. He could hear pain in her voice and wanted to soothe it away, but he'd felt the tremors, too. Probably that was why they were going out to dinner. A big loud show of happiness and solidarity. It's like the big bad wolf trying to blow my house down, Jake thought. There was something out there, something foolish and threatening, and Jake hoped his good solid house of brick could withstand all that huffing and puffing. He drove past George Mason

University and into the town of Fairfax. He turned onto a back street and parked in a small lot, pleased to see there wasn't room for the van.

They walked hand in hand through a quaint alley to the sidewalk and the front of the restaurant. Amy looked down the street at the large white wooden town hall that had been converted into a library. The Wiley house was just across from them, its front yard neatly divided into rectangles by staked string, evidence of historical excavation. Fairfax was an old town, founded by Lord Fairfax, and it had preserved much of its colonial character. Amy liked that. It gave her a feeling of stability and permanence.

Jake guided her into a restaurant that might easily be overlooked by an unknowing passerby. It was a brick row house with ornate white window moldings and an elaborate white portico. The only advertisement was an engraved gold plaque on the door, which stated that this was "Daley's Tavern."

The interior was divided into several small dining rooms, elegantly decorated in eighteenth-century Chippendale and Queen Anne. Amy barely had time to admire the fresh cut flowers in the cool lobby before they were shown to an intimate corner table with a view of the tiny backyard garden. "It's lovely," Amy said.

Jake relaxed into his cherrywood side chair. He agreed. It was lovely, and it was far removed from dancing roosters and canceled castrations. He hadn't realized how badly he'd needed a break from the great chicken caper until they'd entered Daley's.

There was sanity in Daley's. People were sitting in ten miles of bumper-to-bumper traffic on I-95, and they were standing twenty deep at the checkout of the Gourmet Giant supermarket. He, on the other hand, had the good sense to come to Daley's. He felt his eyes glaze over in smug complacency. Daley's was an island in the sea of suburban frenzy. It was calm. It was cool. It was conducive to pleasant conversation.

He looked at the menu and ordered grilled fish. Amy ordered the same. The formally dressed waiter brought them an assortment of warm muffins and breads and a small tub of whipped butter.

Amy buttered a pumpkin muffin and chewed it thoughtfully. "You know what we should do? We should trail Veronica Bottles just like that van is trailing me. Stick to her like glue. Maybe she's got Red stuck away somewhere. Maybe . . ."

Jake made a strangled sound in his throat.

Amy's eyes widened. "What's the matter? You sound like Mrs. Jennings's cat when she coughed up that hairball."

"You weren't supposed to be thinking about Red," he said. "This is supposed to be a romantic interlude. We're supposed to think about love and sex."

"Oh." She nibbled on her muffin. If she thought about sex, she might jump across the table after him. He was incredibly handsome in a navy blazer and blue shirt with red striped tie. His dark lashes shadowed his eyes in the subdued lighting of the room, and there was the hint of a rakish smile at the corners of his mouth, as if he knew a wicked secret. It was a smile that sent a rush of heat tingling through her. She returned the muffin to her bread dish and rearranged her napkin, waiting for the desire to subside. "Well, what about love?"

"Is that what you were just thinking about? Love?"

Amy busily buttered a second pumpkin muffin. "Yup. I was thinking about love. I was thinking that it's . . . um, lovely."

"I was thinking about sex," Jake said, his voice low but casual.

No kidding. Amy grimaced when she realized she'd buttered her thumb.

The waiter placed a shallow bowl of cold zucchini soup before each of them and smiled pleasantly. "Everything all right?"

"Perfect," Jake said, his eyes never leaving Amy's.

When the waiter had retreated Amy shook her bread knife at Jake. "You're seducing me in a public restaurant. Shame on you."

"Is it fun?"

"It's outrageous and excruciating."

He took her hand, rubbing his thumb across the tender flesh of her palm. "Do we need a big wedding? Can we get married tomorrow?"

Amy averted her eyes and tasted her soup. Marry him *now*, instinct told her. Before it's too late. That's insane, she retorted. Nothing's going to happen.

"Amy?"

She gave herself a mental shake. "A big wedding isn't necessary, but I'm sure my parents would want to attend." Her face brightened. "We could have the wedding in my house. Just a few family members and close friends." It would be wonderful, Amy thought. She would fill the house with spring flowers and wear a tea-length dress. Something lacy and Victorian and incredibly romantic. And afterward they could go outdoors for champagne and petit-fours. Thousands of elaborately decorated petit-fours.

Amy was distracted by voices being raised in the next room. The voices grew louder, the twenty-minute men appeared in the doorway, and Amy felt as if her heart had just been freeze-dried. She stared at the men in grim fascination as they approached her table with the minicam running.

"This is Amy Klasse," Ponytail's assistant narrated, "better known as Lulu the Clown . . ."

"Ignore them," Jake said. "Eat your soup."

The newsman continued: ". . . and Dr. Jacob Elliott, owner of the veterinary clinic where Rhode Island Red was mysteriously taken from his small cage."

Jake kept his eyes on his soup, but Amy could see a flush rising from his shirt collar, darkening under his tan. "Ignore them," she mumbled. "Eat your soup."

"Dr. Elliott, this is a very expensive, very romantic restaurant. Am I right in assuming Miss Klasse is more than an ordinary employee?"

Jake coolly stared into the camera lens. "Absolutely. There's nothing ordinary about Miss Klasse."

The man persisted. "We've been told from reliable sources that Miss Klasse is under suspicion for the abduction of the rooster. That, in fact, the police searched her garbage for evidence. Is that correct?"

Jake sighed, took his napkin from his lap, and laid it beside his plate. "You aren't going to give up, are you?"

Ponytail grinned malevolently. "No."

"Excuse me," Jake said, suddenly standing, taking the smaller cameraman by surprise. In one quick movement Jake lifted the minicam from Ponytail's shoulder, removed the microphone, and deposited it in a nearby glass of Burgundy; then he took a swipe at the butter tub, spreading a thick layer of grease on the camera lens. He carefully handed the minicam back to its owner and returned to his seat.

"What do you think of the soup?" he asked Amy.

Ponytail muttered an oath and snatched his microphone from the glass of wine. His eyes were small and glittery. His breath whistled from between bared teeth.

Rodent, Amy thought with a shiver, the man's mousy, dirty-blond hair fueling the comparison. "He looks rabid," she whispered to Jake.

Ponytail reached across the table, grabbed Jake's tie, and plunged it into his zucchini soup. Jake looked at the tie in controlled resignation.

"I'm going to stop wearing ties," he said, blotting at it with his napkin. "This is getting boring."

"I'm going to ruin you and your little friend here," the enraged cameraman ground out. "I'm gonna nail your hide to the wall."

"Don't mess with me," Jake said levelly. "I specialize in neutering."

Two uniformed policemen strode into the dining room accompanied by a glowering headwaiter.

"I'm pressing charges," Ponytail said. "This . . . veterinarian willfully destroyed an expensive microphone."

The officer looked at Jake apologetically. "Maybe you'd better come back to the station house with us."

Amy held out her hands. "I'm going too. Do you want to handcuff me?"

"No ma'am," the policeman said. "I don't think you look dangerous."

Jake stood and helped Amy to her feet. "A lot you know," he said to the smiling policeman.

Outside the restaurant a crowd had gathered around the squad car. Amy faltered a moment when she saw the number of people who had been drawn by the flashing lights on the black-and-white. The crowd parted as the curious parade marched from the restaurant. Two policemen, Lulu the Clown, Jake the veterinarian, and the twenty-minute men complete with battery pack and video. One of the officers helped Amy into the back of the squad car.

Amy clasped her hands in her lap and swallowed back tears. She was disgraced. Publicly humiliated. Plucked from the ritzy restaurant like an undesirable fugitive.

And if that wasn't bad enough, the restaurant was just three doors down from the *Times* office. Without a shadow of a doubt, at least one of those people in the crowd had been a reporter. Tomorrow there would be more newspaper pictures. She could imagine the headlines. "Lulu Arrested with Lover Accomplice."

Two hours later Amy and Jake were back in the little red sports car. "That wasn't so bad," Jake said. "They didn't even arrest us."

Amy took little solace in that fact. There'd been a horde of photographers everywhere she'd gone. She couldn't blame them. She was news. Human interest in a bizarre sort of way.

Jake wistfully looked at the restaurant. "You think they held our table?"

"I think they've probably burned our table."

"Didn't feel like eating fish, anyway. How about a burger?"

"As long as I don't have to get out of the car. If one more person clucks or cock-a-doodles at me I'm going to commit mayhem."

"I know the perfect place. We'll go to the McDrive-in. We'll get McFries, McShakes, McBurgers, and McCookies." He pulled into the drive-through and shouted his order into the order machine. He grinned at Amy. "Is this romantic enough for you?"

Amy had to smile with him. He was invincible. He'd joked with the policemen and jollied her through the entire ordeal. He'd proudly announced their engagement to every passerby, newsmen included. In fact, he seemed to be not at all bothered by the fact that his life was going down the toilet.

Nothing had gone right since he'd known her, she silently wailed. He'd ruined two ties, pitched himself into a Dumpster, been made a public spectacle, almost been arrested, and had his reputation slandered. This wasn't going well. They weren't just talking tremors here. They were looking at earthquake-quality vibes. She shrank back into the seat when Jake reached for the bag of food.

The girl behind the counter leaned out the drive-through window. "Hey, aren't you the lady who cooks chickens? Like wow. Like omigod."

Amy smiled weakly and nodded acknowledgment as Jake stepped on the gas and turned the car toward Main Street. "You're getting quite a following. I never thought I'd have a wife who was famous," he said, reaching for his chocolate shake.

"I think the word is infamous. I feel like Lizzie Borden."

Jake took a long pull on the straw. She was mustering up a reasonable amount of bravado, but under it all she was really hurting, and he wasn't sure exactly why. Part of it was a sense of responsibility to maintain a certain image for the children who had watched her, but it had to be more than that. She'd looked like an angel in the police station with her blond curls and serious wide blue eyes, responding politely to everyone. A credit to her acting ability, he'd thought, remembering the few unguarded moments when the facade had slipped, and she'd seemed so lost. Almost victimized. Like a piece of driftwood, floating downstream, unable to control its journey.

He snitched a french fry while he waited for a light. It was always dangerous to second-guess someone. Maybe he was reading too much into this. She'd led a very law-abiding, sheltered life. Maybe she'd just been overwhelmed by the police station. He didn't want to be insensitive, but he also didn't want to make more of this than it was. Hell, maybe they should just move to Arizona and start over.

They finished their meal on the back porch, topping it off with fresh strawberries and ice cream, watching the night sky spread a calming blackness over the earth. Jake played with the ruffle on Amy's sleeve. "Is there something you'd like to talk about?"

She didn't want to talk. She didn't want to think. She was afraid if she thought too clearly, she'd have to make painful decisions, so she kept her eyes on the oak tree at the far perimeter of her yard. Its trunk was thick and gnarled; its branches spanned the house. A survivor, Amy decided. It had eluded the bulldozers that had leveled the land in preparation for her housing development. It had been in the appropriate place: a small swale between two lots. Perhaps that was her problem . . . she was never in the appropriate place.

A warm breeze moved through the leaves, producing a hypnotic clacking sound. She felt Jake's fingers at the nape of her neck, stroking, caressing. She closed her eyes and gave herself up to the pleasure of his touch, a lovely lethargy taking possession of her. Jake always knew how to make her feel better.

Chapter 9

Rain. As if she wasn't depressed enough, it had to rain. Not even a healthy rain that could be considered cozy, pattering on leaves and window-panes. This rain drizzled. Gray, dreary drizzle. Amy pressed her fingertips to her eyelids. She didn't think she could face another day.

She listened to Jake singing in the shower and narrowed her eyes. He had a lot of nerve waking up happy. Little Miss Mary Sunshine. He wasn't Miss Mary Sunshine last night when he told her the pot roast was dry. And he wasn't Miss Mary Sunshine at the office when she couldn't find a file. Nobody was Mary Sunshine at the office. Everybody was walking around like their shorts were too tight.

It was almost a week since the damn rooster had gotten snatched and the customers were still uncomfortable. The boarding cages were empty, and Jake was eating so many doughnuts he couldn't button his shirt. She flopped over onto her stomach and buried her face in the pillow. "Ugh."

Jake strolled into the bedroom, dropped his towel, and pulled on a pair of freshly laundered briefs and jeans. He grabbed the lump under the quilt that was Amy's toe. "Get up, lazy bones. You'll be late for work."

She stuck her lower lip out and scowled. "I'm not going to work today."

Jake shrugged into his shirt. "We've been all through this. You weren't going to work yesterday, either."

"And you talked me into it, and it was a mistake."

Jake looked wounded. "How can you say it was a mistake? What about lunch hour when we made love in the lavatory?"

"We made love in the lavatory because we were hiding from that group of animal rights activists camped out in the parking lot! The ones who hanged Lulu in effigy."

Jake tugged on a pair of argyle socks and slid his feet into new loafers. "They won't be back today. They're picketing the White House."

Amy got out of bed and stomped off to the kitchen. "I suppose you got that information from the cute little redhead who was young enough to be your daughter!"

Jake grinned at her. "You're jealous."

Amy put the teakettle on to boil. "I'm *not* jealous. I'm insecure, immature, ungrateful, and unemployed. I quit."

"You can't quit."

"Watch me." She poked a finger into his chest. "I can do whatever I want, buster, and I want to quit."

"Know what I think?" Jake taunted. "I think you're . . . chicken."

"That's not funny. You have a perverted sense of humor."

"At least I'm not crabby."

Amy's eyes widened. "Are you telling me I'm crabby?"

"Damn right you're crabby. And you're stubborn."

"That does it," Amy said. "I'm leaving."

"Good. Where are you going? I hope it's to work, because we're already late and Mr. Billings is coming in this morning."

"Read my lips, Elliott. I quit. I'm good-bye. Adios. Au revoir."

Jake looked at the kitchen clock and sighed. "I have to go. We'll discuss this later."

"My mind is made up."

"Stubborn," Jake mumbled en route to the front door. "Damn stubborn woman. Enough to drive a man nuts." He returned to the kitchen and grabbed Amy, kissing her long and hard. His eyes briefly fogged over with pleasure before he sighed for the second time that morning and left. Elliott, he said to himself, she's got you by the short hairs.

Amy listened to the door slam and the car sputter to life. She glowered at the cat, sitting patiently by the refrigerator door. "I suppose you want to get fed?" She took the cat food from the refrigerator and dumped it into a bowl. Motley sniffed at it disdainfully. Amy couldn't really blame her. The stuff smelled gross.

"You're gonna love this," Amy said with a voice sweet enough to draw ants. "This cat food is great stuff. It says here under guaranteed analysis that there's eleven percent of crude protein, six percent of crude fat, and one percent fiber. And this is the really important part. Two percent ash. How about that?"

Motley didn't look impressed. Amy added a dollop of vanilla ice cream to the top of the cat food and watched Motley's eyes light up.

"Know what, Motley? We've got to go. Jake's right. I'm crabby. I'm not marriage material. I'm having a stress attack."

She made herself a cup of tea and sat at the kitchen table calmly thinking about her life. She needed to get away. Being Jake's receptionist wasn't working out. She wasn't even sure if being Jake's fiancée was working out. She loved him, but love might not be enough.

Sometimes there were insurmountable problems. Rhode Island Red seemed to be one of them. What she needed now was a hideout. Someplace quiet and uncomplicated where she could lick her wounds and make some intelligent decisions. She had an aunt in Baltimore. Maybe a visit with Aunt Gert would be just what she needed. And Baltimore might even be a good place to look for a job. Her fame might not have spread to Baltimore.

"Depressing," she said to Motley. "This whole thing is damn depressing."

Amy finished her tea and dragged herself into the shower, turning the water on full force, letting it beat down on her shoulders. An overwhelming sadness constricted her throat, and she felt hot tears streaming down her cheeks, despite all efforts at controlling them. Love is the pits, she thought, slumping against the tile and sobbing, for the first time in her life understanding the term *heartbroken*. Why couldn't it have worked just this once? Jake was the man of her dreams and Rhode Island Red had turned those dreams into a nightmare.

An hour later she taped a note to the refrigerator door. *Dear Jake, Had to leave. Please water my plants.*

Love, Amy. She stared dully at the note. It was inadequate, but then life itself seemed inadequate right now. Maybe the note was appropriate. She'd crammed almost all of her clothes into the small car. Motley was waiting in the cat carrier on the front seat. Jake had his own house key. Nothing more left to do.

Jake threw the day's paper on the unmade bed and zapped the TV with the remote. Five days since Amy left and not a word. It was crazy. She'd vanished. Poof. Just like Red. He was beginning to have weird thoughts, like, maybe the same people who took Red also took Amy. Maybe Amy had actually been the one who took Red and they were holed up in a motel room somewhere, together.

You're a man on the edge, Jake, he told himself. You're getting silly. Better silly than frantic, he decided. That's how he actually felt deep down inside. Total panic. She was gone, and he couldn't find her. What if she never came back?

Of course she'd come back. She was Ms. Responsibility. She'd come back to get her mail and pay her bills. She'd come back to retrieve her furniture. Would she come back to him? He kicked off his shoes and fell onto the bed. He didn't even know why she left, and he was mad as hell that she hadn't explained.

She'd owed him an explanation, dammit. If he ever found her he was going to strangle her.

Undoubtedly this had something to do with the rooster mess. He had to admit, it'd been a crummy week. Business was bad. People were snapping at each other. And Amy felt it was all her fault.

He should have seen it coming, but he'd been too busy reassuring skeptical clients to take time to reassure Amy. Then there was that dumb shouting match the morning she'd left. He'd been insensitive, he decided. He hadn't listened to her. She'd said she was leaving, and it had never occurred to him to take her seriously. Elliott, you're a moron.

He flicked through several channels and sat bolt upright when the twenty-minute news show popped onto the screen. ". . . and that's the story, folks. Amy Klasse has disappeared, leaving her fiancé without a word. One can only speculate as to her whereabouts and wonder at her motives."

Jake threw the remote across the room, where it smashed against the wall. They were still at it! Wasn't it enough that they'd driven her away? He banged his fist on the top of the TV and listened to the set crackle and die. Great. Now he was violent. He laced up his running shoes and hooked the leash onto Spot's collar.

"Come on, dog. We need to walk."

It was dawn when Jake stopped walking. He and Spot wearily made their way up the stairs and flopped into bed. An hour later the alarm rang. Jake staggered to the shower.

"Man, this sucks," he said. "I'm falling apart. Look at me . . . I'm even talking to myself. Get a grip, Jake."

He stared at himself in the mirror and didn't like what he saw. Dark circles under his eyes. Two days of stubble. Unkempt hair. He looked like a street person. "You see what falling in love does to you?" he shouted at his reflection. "Women! They'll ruin you. They make you crazy."

He was still raving when he got to the office. Allen was sitting at the reception desk. "We need help," Allen said. "The office is in chaos. I can't find any files. We're overbooked again." He scowled at Jake. "And I hate your damn coffee."

Jake scowled back. "So make your own damn coffee."

"I hate mine even more than I hate yours. I like Amy's coffee. Where the hell is she, anyway?"

Jake made a futile gesture.

Allen slumped in his seat. "I'm sorry. I got carried away. You look like death warmed over. Bad night?"

"Unh."

Allen grinned and draped an arm around Jake's shoulders. "She'll be back. She loves you. And her cat is due for a rabies shot."

Both men stiffened when the door opened and the twenty-minute news team walked in. "Did you see the show?" Ponytail asked. "Pretty good, huh? Real drama. Real pathos."

"Real close to slander," Jake said. "You have a lot of nerve showing up here this morning. I guess you like to live dangerously."

Allen's hand tightened on Jake's shoulder. "Maybe you'd better leave," Allen said. "Dr. Elliott hasn't had his jelly doughnut yet. He can be pretty mean until he gets his jelly doughnut."

Ponytail narrowed his eyes. "Hey, this wasn't our idea. We got a call to come over here."

Jake looked at Allen. "Did you call these slimeballs?"

"Not me."

"It was a woman," Ponytail said. "Real sexy voice, but sounded kind of dumb."

Veronica Bottles minced through the door. "It was me." Her breasts bounced unfettered behind a lime-green tank top as she tottered precariously on spike-heeled shoes. "Is my makeup okay?" she asked Ponytail. "I want to look good on TV."

Ponytail looked surprised. "Who are you?"

Veronica stood tall, her nose slightly tipped toward the ceiling. "Veronica Bottles. I'm an actress, and I was Rhode Island Red's trainer. Red and I were TV stars together." She turned her heavily mascaraed eyes to Jake. "I'm really sorry about everything that's happened. Is it true Lulu's gone?"

Jake nodded.

"Gosh, it must have been love at first sight for you and Lulu. That's so romantic. And so sad. Star-crossed lovers." She sighed.

"I sure hope things work out for you," she said to Jake. "I watched their show last night and I said to myself, Veronica, things have gone too far. Somebody's gotta do something about this rooster business. Gee, people's lives are being ruined. All over a silly old rooster."

She knew about Red. Jake could feel it in his bones. He'd felt it all along, but now he knew. Patience, he cautioned himself. Deep breathing. "Um, do you know something about Red?"

"Of course, I know about Red. He was my rooster, for crying out loud."

She turned to the newsmen. "Red and I were very close. We'd only known each other for a short time, but we were like family. He lived in my apartment, you know."

"About Red," Jake prompted. "I don't suppose you'd know where he is now?"

Veronica blinked her huge black lashes. "I'm not sure. I suppose he's where he's always been. Unless somebody's moved him. I was going to tell you that very first day, but there were all those newsmen and cameras and policemen. It never occurred to me you'd call the police. I mean, he was just a chicken! Then there was Brian Turner, the little weasel."

"Ah ha, Turner was in on this, too. I knew it," Jake said, shaking his finger at Allen.

"After I left Red here I got to feeling sorry for him. I got to thinking about how lonely he must be in a strange cage. Red always liked to watch TV at night and here he was with no one to talk to and no TV to watch. I came back to visit him, but there wasn't anybody here, and the office was all locked up."

"So you used a credit card to get in to see Red," Jake said.

Allen grinned at Jake. "You sound like Maxwell Smart."

"It was easy," Veronica said. "I'm real good with credit cards. I'm always forgetting the keys to my apartment. Anyway, I let myself in the office. I didn't think you'd mind. I even gave all the animals a drink of fresh water before I left."

Jake made an effort to remain calm. "That was nice of you. Getting back to Red . . ."

Veronica's eyes got teary. "He was dead. Poor dumb bird. He was lying in his cage with his little chicken feet sticking up."

"Why didn't you tell us?"

"I meant to, honest. I just didn't get a chance, and then things started happening so fast. Besides, when Lulu brought the chicken soup in, I figured she'd found him."

"What are you talking about? Where *was* he?"

"Well, I didn't think it was right to leave Red in that cage. He was dead. *Real* dead, if you know what I mean." She stuck her arms straight out and puffed up her cheeks. "Bloat city."

Jake bit his lip. Allen made a strange sound in the back of his throat.

Veronica smiled smugly. "Everyone thinks I'm dumb, but I'm not. I'm pretty good at figuring things out. I said to myself, Veronica, what should you do with this smelly chicken? The answer was simple. You treat it like any other chicken. So I wrapped it in aluminum foil and put it in your freezer."

"Omigod. You mean that bird's been in our freezer all this time?"

Veronica looked puzzled. "Unless Lulu used him for soup. I only labeled it *chicken.* I didn't put his name on the package. I stopped back the following night to see if Red was still here, but there was someone in the office. I was afraid it was a burglar, so I drove away and called the police. Then I went to Brian's house and told him about Red, and he almost had a cow. He was yelling and screaming at me, telling me how I was just a chicken killer, and how I was going to ruin his ratings. I thought if Red wasn't already made into soup he deserved a decent burial, but Brian said no, no, no. He said it wouldn't look good. He said I'd get arrested and sent to jail for breaking into the clinic. Then, the next day, the rotten son of a creep fired me."

Jake and Allen looked at each other and simultaneously turned and ran to the small kitchenette. Jake opened the freezer door and extracted the package marked *chicken*. "How could we have missed this?"

Allen shrugged. "I thought Amy had brought it in. She was always bringing us food."

Jake unwrapped the aluminum foil and grimaced. "Veronica, how could you think Amy would make soup out of Red?"

"It did seem pretty weirdo, but you have to admit, it was a strange coincidence for her to bring that soup in."

Jake rewrapped Red and put him back in the freezer. "I don't know whether to laugh or cry."

Veronica turned to Ponytail. "So you see, this was all my fault. It's not right that Dr. Elliott's romance went belly-up." Veronica jiggled a little in her excitement, catching Ponytail's full attention. "I thought, maybe, you could do another show about the real story of Red, and I could be the star. It could be an exposé. We could get that creep Turner where he lives. And Lulu would see the show and come back and everyone would live happily ever after."

Ponytail smiled. "I think that'd be a great idea."

It was a great idea, Jake thought, but what if Amy didn't see it? It was a local cable station. What if Amy was far away? What if she had bigger fish to fry at nine o'clock Friday night? Lord, how he missed her. Especially at night when there was nothing else to occupy his mind, and the bed felt cold and empty next to him. He closed his eyes, but he couldn't sleep. He looked at the digital clock on the nightstand, uttered an expletive, and thrashed under the covers. Two o'clock.

From the foot of the bed, Spot belligerently opened one eye. *Now* what? he seemed to say. Better not be another marathon nocturnal walk.

Jake grunted and reached for the brand-new remote. He punched up a pillow behind himself and sullenly turned on his TV. He flipped through the stations looking for something boring, and settled on a news station from Baltimore.

". . . news and weather *live* from Baltimore, every hour on the hour," a fat little man announced. "And now *here's* the weather."

The camera panned to a slim young woman with tousled blond curls. The woman blinked in an obvious effort to stay awake. "Here's the weather," she mumbled. "It's going to rain. Big deal. Do you care?" She moved to a wall map of the United States and pointed to Kansas. "There's a high over the Great Lakes." She moved the pointer to Florida. "And a storm front coming in from the Rockies." She squinted into the camera. "Is anybody out there?"

Jake had stopped breathing. It was Amy. Coming to him live, every hour on the hour, from Baltimore. The worst weather girl in the history of television. Out on her feet and cranky. His lips curved in a stiff smile.

Two hours later Jake found the station and parked next to Amy's red car. It was a small operation. Not much more than a warehouse in a light industrial complex. The night watchman directed Jake to a door at the end of a short hall.

"Be quiet," he said, "it's time for the news. It's live, you know. And watch out for the weather girl. She's not used to keeping these hours. She's a little . . . accident prone."

Jake silently eased into the shadows at the back of the room. The dirty cement floor was littered with used coffee cups and cigarette butts. Ten or twelve tan folding chairs had been set up for an audience that didn't exist. Two cameras focused on the brightly lit platform against the far wall. A shelf-type desk with a blue bunting skirt occupied half of the platform, the blue screen the other half. A little man with a perfectly round face sat at one end of the desk.

Amy sat at the end closest to the screen, staring steely-eyed at a spot on the desktop. She was tired. Physically tired and emotionally tired. She missed Jake. She'd moved from place to place throughout her entire childhood, leaving people and places she'd loved, but she'd never experienced anything like this. This was agony. Empty, desperate, incomprehensible agony.

She lived in a constant haze of painful longing, wondering what Jake was doing, if he was well, if he thought of her. It had only been a week, she told herself. Could that be possible? She could barely remember the reasons for leaving. Something foolish about his business and clairvoyant vibrations.

No, that wasn't really it. Be honest, Amy. She'd bailed out when the going got tough. That was the worst of the pain. No faith in their love. No guts. It wasn't like her. Why had she been so weak just at the time when she should have been strong?

She was going back on Saturday to try to make amends, but first she had to sleep. If only she could sleep for more than an hour at a time . . .

". . . and now here's the treat you've all been waiting for, Amy Klasse with the weather."

Amy smiled at the announcer. "Thank you, Ed."

There was a guffaw from one of the cameramen. "His name's *Ben*," he said in a stage whisper.

Amy sighed. "Thank you, Ben. Well everybody, the weather hasn't changed any since three o'clock. It's . . . um, it's nice out. And it's dark." Her eyes slid closed and she gave herself a small shake. "About the map. Here it is," she said, gesturing with the pointer. "It's got weather all over it."

The red light winked off the camera, and the cameraman called, "Cut." Amy slumped in her seat. "How do you ever get used to this? How do you guys stay awake all night?"

"Don't worry about it," the cameraman said. "You're doing great. People are actually staying up to see you mumble through the weather and demolish the set. They especially liked the time you caught your heel in the desk skirt and trashed the whole platform."

The round-faced man grinned at Amy. "Our ratings are going up because of you. People think you're funny."

Amy returned the smile, but it didn't extend to her eyes. There was a numbness to her face that went beyond exhaustion. Even her curls seemed limp.

"Thanks for being so nice to me," she said. "See you guys tomorrow."

She slung her purse over her shoulder and bumped into Jake. "Oops, 'scuse me." She took a step backward. "Omigod."

There was a moment of tension-filled silence. "Surprise," Jake said, low and threatening.

"How did you find me?"

Jake ran his finger along the collar of her shirt. "I saw you on television. I've been having trouble sleeping lately."

Suddenly Amy was wide awake.

He turned her chin up with his finger. "I think you have some explaining to do."

Amy swallowed. Who was this man? Freshly showered, dark hair, darker eyes. Black T-shirt casually molded to broad shoulders and flat stomach. Jeans stretched tight across slim hips and a perfect butt. She was falling apart, and Jacob Elliott was standing in front of her radiating enough health and virility to make her shoes smoke.

She'd imagined this moment a million times in the past eight days. Never like this. He was supposed to be distraught, with dark circles under his eyes. Or angry . . . sullen and silent, the brooding phase. Or ecstatically happy, instantly realizing that they were reunited forever and ever.

Jake wasn't any of those. He was . . . enigmatic. She'd thought that was a term only romance writers used, but there he was with unreadable eyes the color of strong coffee, and a mouth that held a hint of amused satisfaction, a mouth that promised . . . what? Damn. She licked dry lips and felt like a small, tasty animal being stalked by a large, sleek cat.

"Time to go home, Amy. We have unfinished business."

"I'm living with my aunt Gert. She's—"

"Not tonight." He took her by the elbow and steered her toward the door.

Amy pulled away. "Now, just a darn minute! You can't come riding in here doing your John Wayne impression and expect me to fawn at your feet."

"No?"

She stuck her chin out pugnaciously. "No. I'll be the first one to admit I owe you an explanation, and I'll be happy to provide it in the morning." It wasn't the sort of thing she wanted to do on an empty stomach, exhausted and unshowered. She needed makeup. This was an explanation that required eyeliner and the expensive moisturizer.

"Guess again," Jake said, his hand at the small of her back, guiding her through the parking lot to a car that made hers look like a toy. It was black and racy and low to the ground, shining with malevolent power and elegance in the dimly lit lot. The sort of car James Bond would drive.

Jake opened the door to the passenger side and Amy was enveloped by the smell of new car and expensive leather. She took a step backward and looked at Jake warily. "What's this?"

"New car," he said matter-of-factly. "My old car died."

He made a gallant motion for her to get in.

He drove through Baltimore and turned onto I-95 South. He looked at her sideways, a silent speculative assessment that sent a shiver running down her spine.

The radial tires sang over the pavement, the powerful engine droned in her ears, hypnotic and soothing, and she closed her eyes to Jake, suddenly too tired to think.

She barely roused herself when the car purred to a stop. She was lifted from her seat and carried. A wave of fresh morning air washed over her and then there was the still coolness of air-conditioning. She opened her eyes when she was gently laid on her bed, but immediately gave herself up to the delicious luxury of smooth sheets and soft quilts.

Jake drew the curtains in Amy's bedroom and stared down at her sleeping form.

It was noon before Amy awoke. Her first thought was that she was home. Her second thought was that Jake was naked beside her, his warm hand resting on a very private place.

They made love and when they were done, he snuggled her against him.

"I suppose we should talk now."

Amy cuddled next to him. "I don't know. It seems to me we've just said it all."

Jake cocked an inquisitive eyebrow at her. "Me, man . . . you, woman?"

"Something like that. I was thinking more along the lines of you, Mr. Elliott . . . me, Mrs. Elliott."

"Lady"—Jake grinned—"you're in luck. I have a cancellation this afternoon."